— William Shakespeare's —

Othello

adapted by **Vincent Goodwin**
illustrated by **Chris Allen**

visit us at
www.abdopublishing.com

Published by Magic Wagon, a division of the ABDO Publishing Group, 8000 West 78th Street, Edina, Minnesota 55439. Copyright © 2009 by Abdo Consulting Group, Inc. International copyrights reserved in all countries. All rights reserved. No part of this book may be reproduced in any form without written permission from the publisher.
Graphic Planet™ is a trademark and logo of Magic Wagon.

Printed in the United States.

Adapted by Vincent Goodwin
Illustrated by Chris Allen
Edited by Stephanie Hedlund and Rochelle Baltzer
Interior layout and design by Antarctic Press
Cover art by Chris Allen
Cover design by Neil Klinepier

Library of Congress Cataloging-in-Publication Data

Goodwin, Vincent
    William Shakespeare's Othello / adapted by Vincent Goodwin; illustrated by Chris Allen.
       p. cm. -- (Graphic Shakespeare)
    Summary: Retells, in comic book format, Shakespeare's play in which a jealous general is duped into thinking that his wife has been unfaithful, with tragic consequences.
    ISBN 978-1-60270-192-2
    1. Graphic novels. [1. Graphic novels. 2. Shakespeare, William, 1564-1616--Adaptations.]
    I. Allen, Chris, 1972- ill. II. Shakespeare, William, 1564-1616. Othello. III. Title. IV. Title: Othello.

PZ7.7.G66Wg 2008
741.5'973--dc22

                                    2008010743

Table of Contents

Cast of Characters

Othello
The Moor

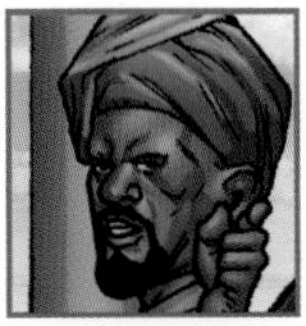

Brabantio
Father to Desdemona

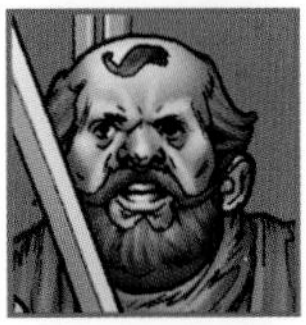

Cassio
An honorable lieutenant

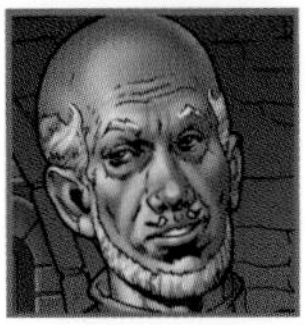

Iago
A villain

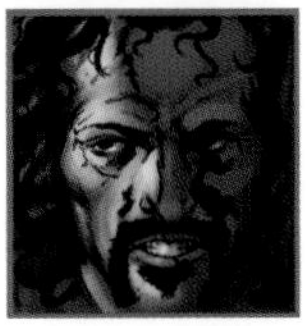

Roderigo
A gentleman

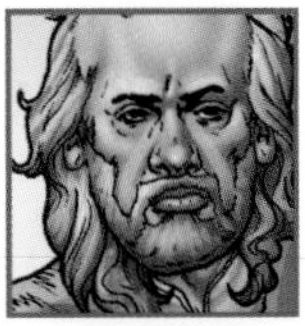

Duke of Venice

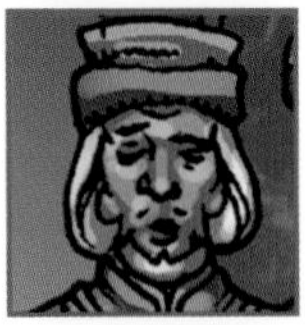

Montano
Governor of Cyprus

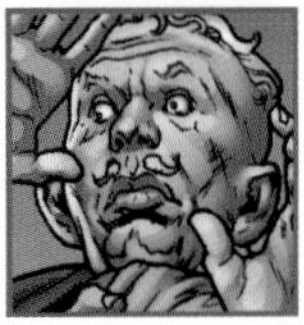

Lodovico
Noble Venetian

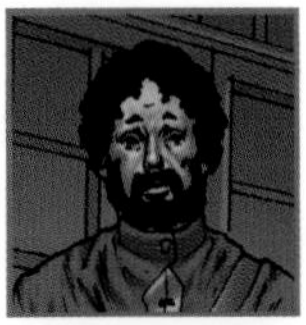

Gatiano
Noble Venetian

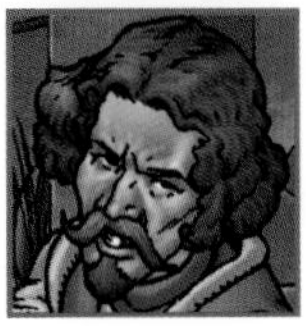

Desdemona
Wife to Othello

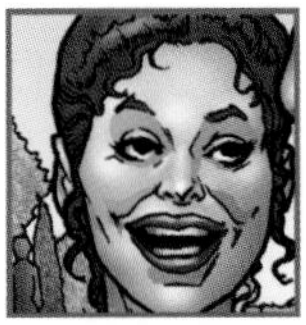

Emilia
Wife to Iago

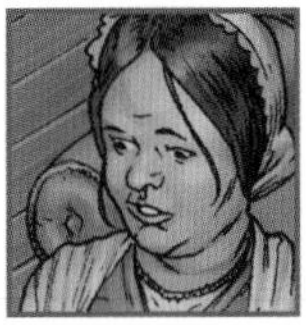

Our Setting

The first act of *Othello* is set in Venice, Italy. The rest of the play is set on the island of Cyprus. Venice is located in northeastern Italy. The city lies on about 120 islands in the Adriatic Sea.

Venice became an important trading center as early as the AD 800s. During late medieval times, the city was the greatest seaport in Europe. Venice served as Europe's commercial and cultural link with Asia. Ships from Venice carried almost all the silks, spices, and other luxury items to Europe from Asia.

Cyprus is an island in the eastern Mediterranean Sea. It is best known for its mineral wealth, wines and produce, and natural beauty. The island has always been an important trading post between Europe, Africa, and the Middle East.

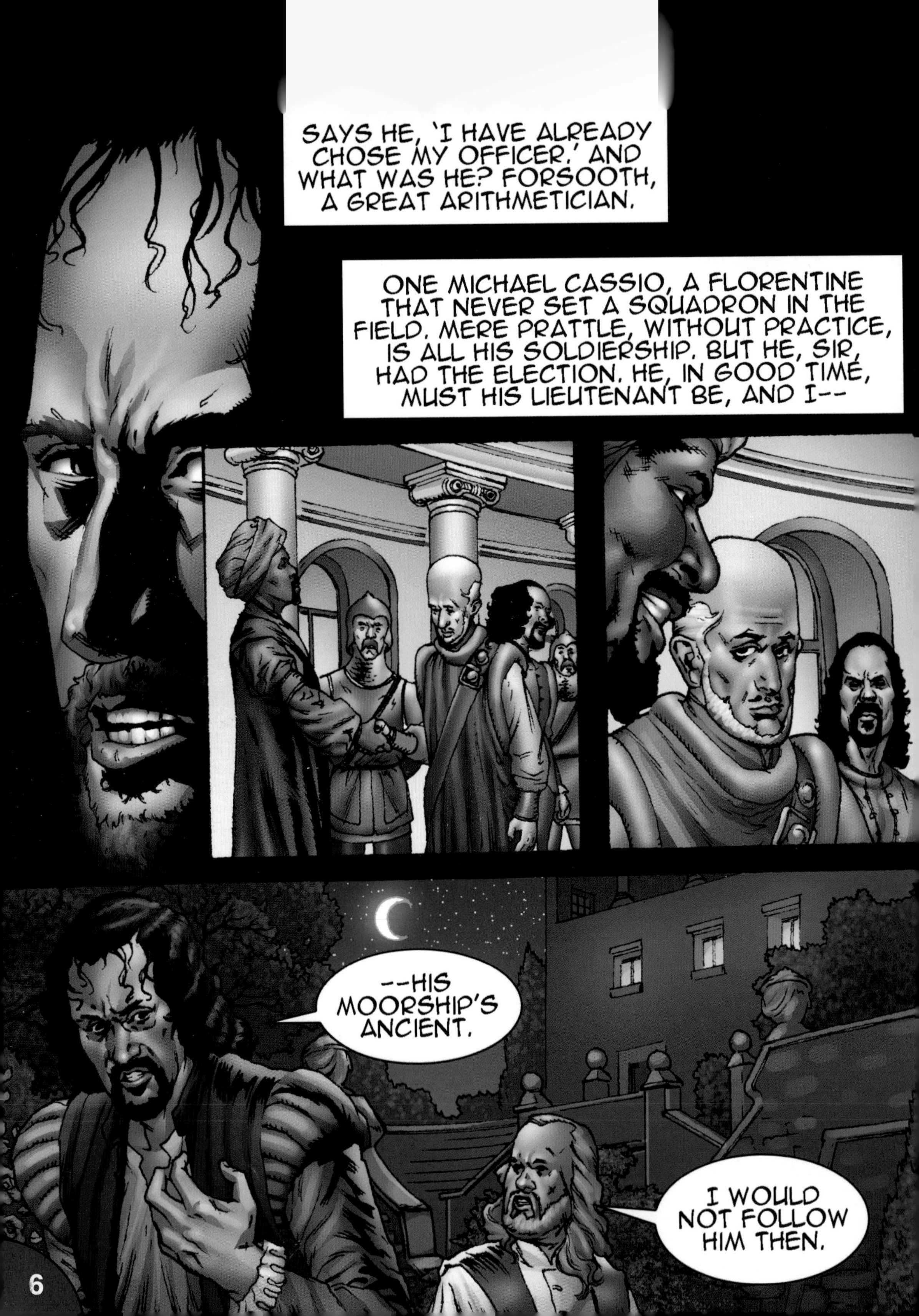
SAYS HE, 'I HAVE ALREADY CHOSE MY OFFICER.' AND WHAT WAS HE? FORSOOTH, A GREAT ARITHMETICIAN.
ONE MICHAEL CASSIO, A FLORENTINE THAT NEVER SET A SQUADRON IN THE FIELD. MERE PRATTLE, WITHOUT PRACTICE, IS ALL HIS SOLDIERSHIP. BUT HE, SIR, HAD THE ELECTION. HE, IN GOOD TIME, MUST HIS LIEUTENANT BE, AND I--
--HIS MOORSHIP'S ANCIENT.
I WOULD NOT FOLLOW HIM THEN.

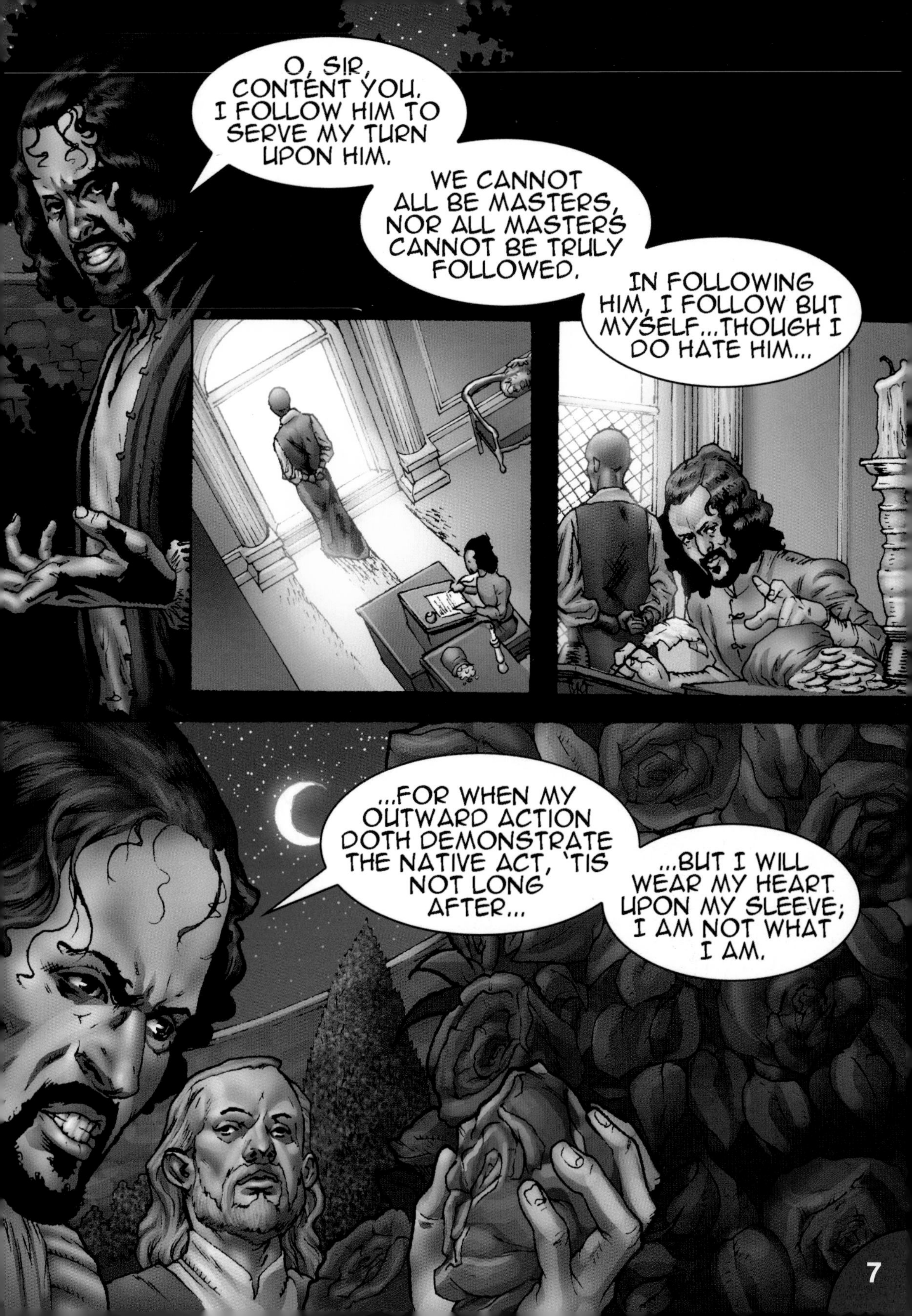
O, SIR, CONTENT YOU. I FOLLOW HIM TO SERVE MY TURN UPON HIM.
WE CANNOT ALL BE MASTERS, NOR ALL MASTERS CANNOT BE TRULY FOLLOWED.
IN FOLLOWING HIM, I FOLLOW BUT MYSELF...THOUGH I DO HATE HIM...
...FOR WHEN MY OUTWARD ACTION DOTH DEMONSTRATE THE NATIVE ACT, 'TIS NOT LONG AFTER...
...BUT I WILL WEAR MY HEART UPON MY SLEEVE; I AM NOT WHAT I AM.

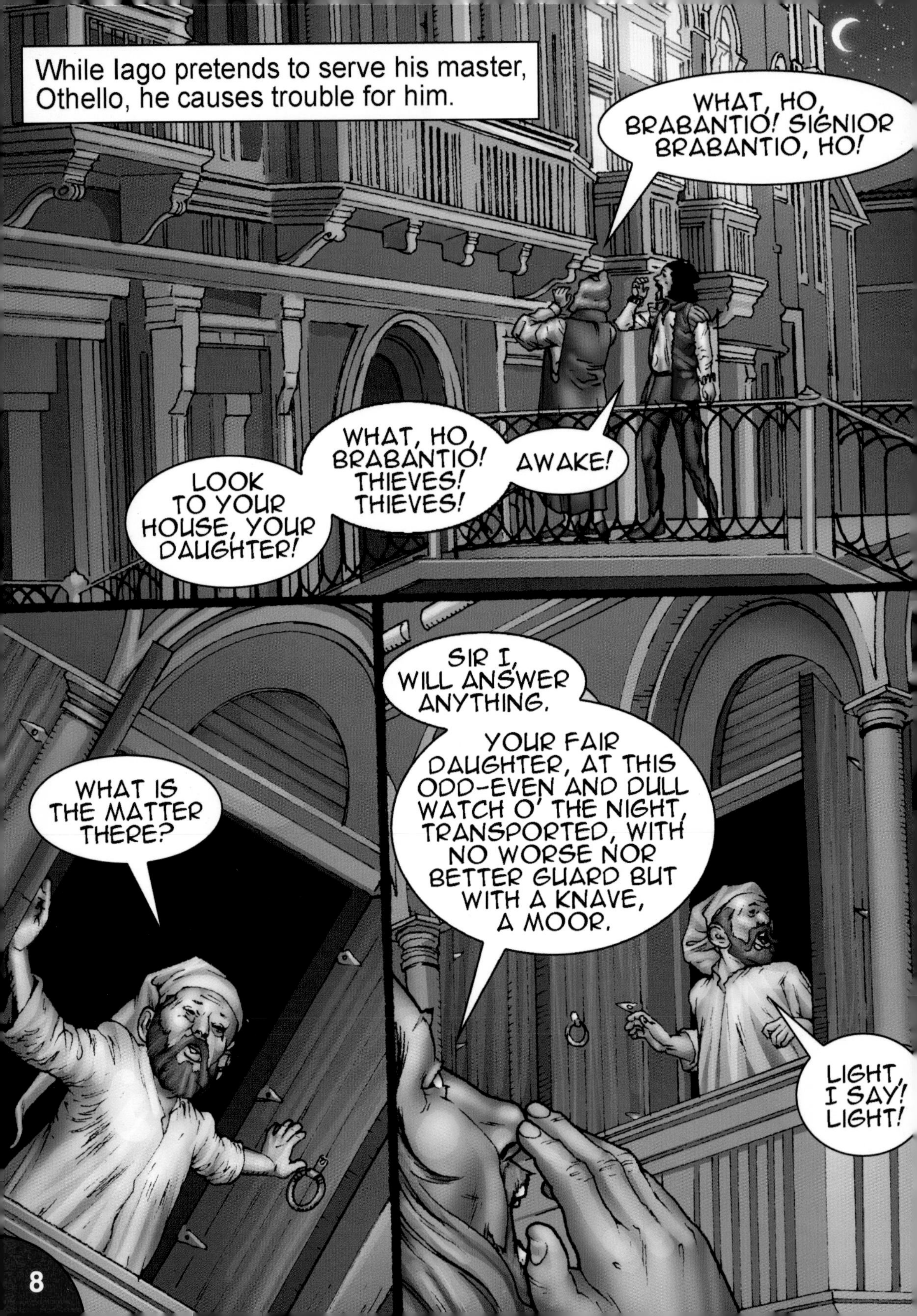
While Iago pretends to serve his master, Othello, he causes trouble for him.
WHAT, HO, BRABANTIO! SIGNIOR BRABANTIO, HO!
AWAKE!
WHAT, HO, BRABANTIO! THIEVES! THIEVES!
LOOK TO YOUR HOUSE, YOUR DAUGHTER!
WHAT IS THE MATTER THERE?
SIR I, WILL ANSWER ANYTHING.
YOUR FAIR DAUGHTER, AT THIS ODD-EVEN AND DULL WATCH O' THE NIGHT, TRANSPORTED, WITH NO WORSE NOR BETTER GUARD BUT WITH A KNAVE, A MOOR.
LIGHT, I SAY! LIGHT!

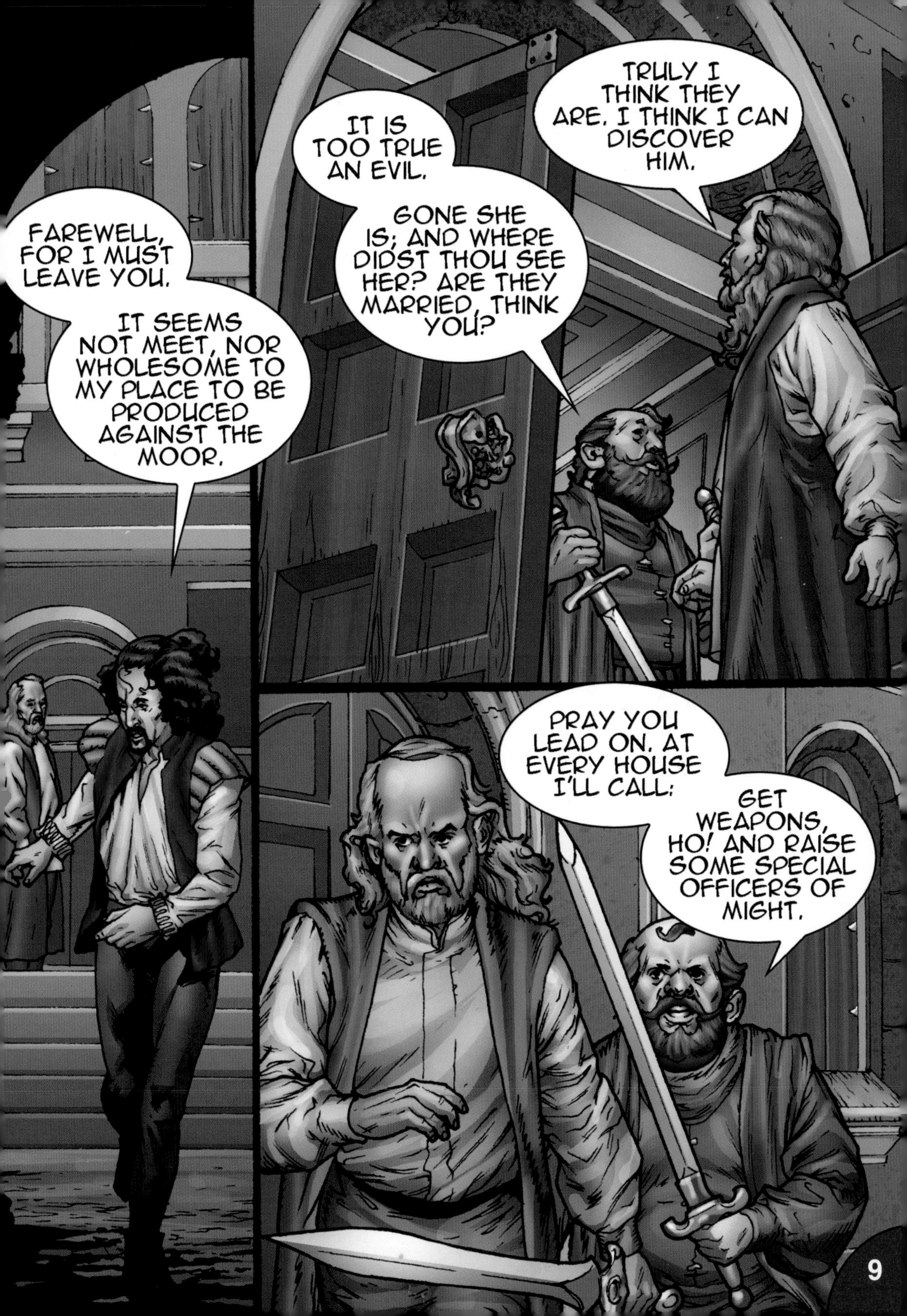
FAREWELL, FOR I MUST LEAVE YOU.
IT SEEMS NOT MEET, NOR WHOLESOME TO MY PLACE TO BE PRODUCED AGAINST THE MOOR.
IT IS TOO TRUE AN EVIL.
GONE SHE IS; AND WHERE DIDST THOU SEE HER? ARE THEY MARRIED, THINK YOU?
TRULY I THINK THEY ARE. I THINK I CAN DISCOVER HIM.
PRAY YOU LEAD ON. AT EVERY HOUSE I'LL CALL:
GET WEAPONS, HO! AND RAISE SOME SPECIAL OFFICERS OF MIGHT.

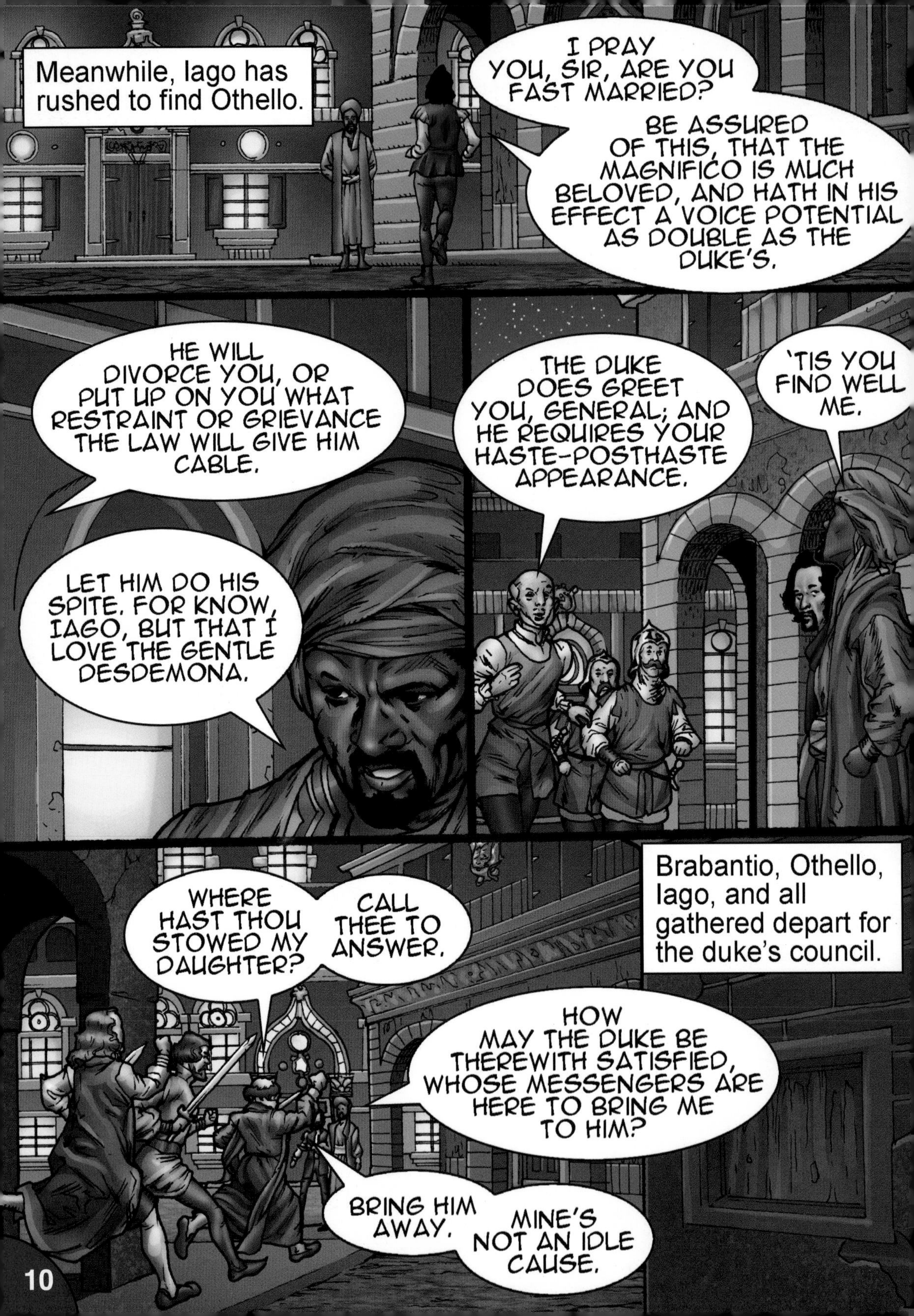
Meanwhile, Iago has rushed to find Othello.
I PRAY YOU, SIR, ARE YOU FAST MARRIED?
BE ASSURED OF THIS, THAT THE MAGNIFICO IS MUCH BELOVED, AND HATH IN HIS EFFECT A VOICE POTENTIAL AS DOUBLE AS THE DUKE'S.
HE WILL DIVORCE YOU, OR PUT UP ON YOU WHAT RESTRAINT OR GRIEVANCE THE LAW WILL GIVE HIM CABLE.
LET HIM DO HIS SPITE. FOR KNOW, IAGO, BUT THAT I LOVE THE GENTLE DESDEMONA.
THE DUKE DOES GREET YOU, GENERAL; AND HE REQUIRES YOUR HASTE-POSTHASTE APPEARANCE.
'TIS YOU FIND WELL ME.
Brabantio, Othello, Iago, and all gathered depart for the duke's council.
WHERE HAST THOU STOWED MY DAUGHTER?
CALL THEE TO ANSWER.
HOW MAY THE DUKE BE THEREWITH SATISFIED, WHOSE MESSENGERS ARE HERE TO BRING ME TO HIM?
BRING HIM AWAY.
MINE'S NOT AN IDLE CAUSE.

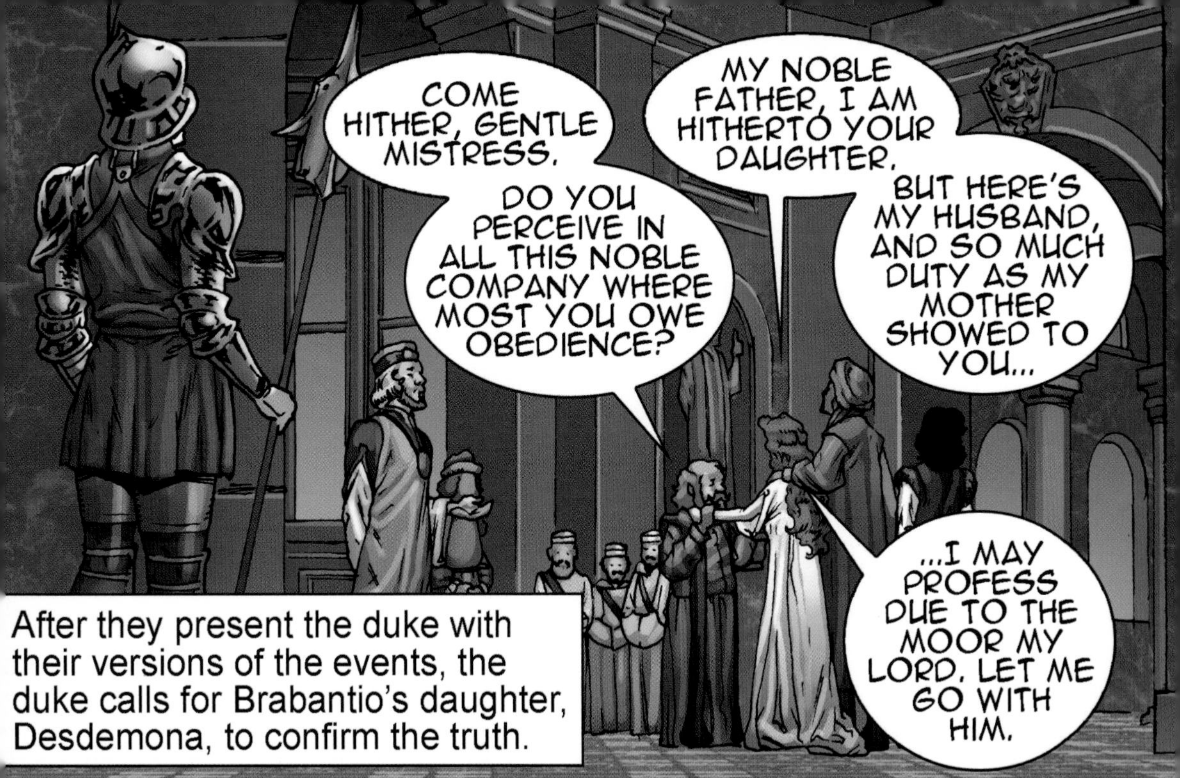
After they present the duke with their versions of the events, the duke calls for Brabantio's daughter, Desdemona, to confirm the truth.
COME HITHER, GENTLE MISTRESS.
DO YOU PERCEIVE IN ALL THIS NOBLE COMPANY WHERE MOST YOU OWE OBEDIENCE?
MY NOBLE FATHER, I AM HITHERTO YOUR DAUGHTER.
BUT HERE'S MY HUSBAND, AND SO MUCH DUTY AS MY MOTHER SHOWED TO YOU...
...I MAY PROFESS DUE TO THE MOOR MY LORD. LET ME GO WITH HIM.

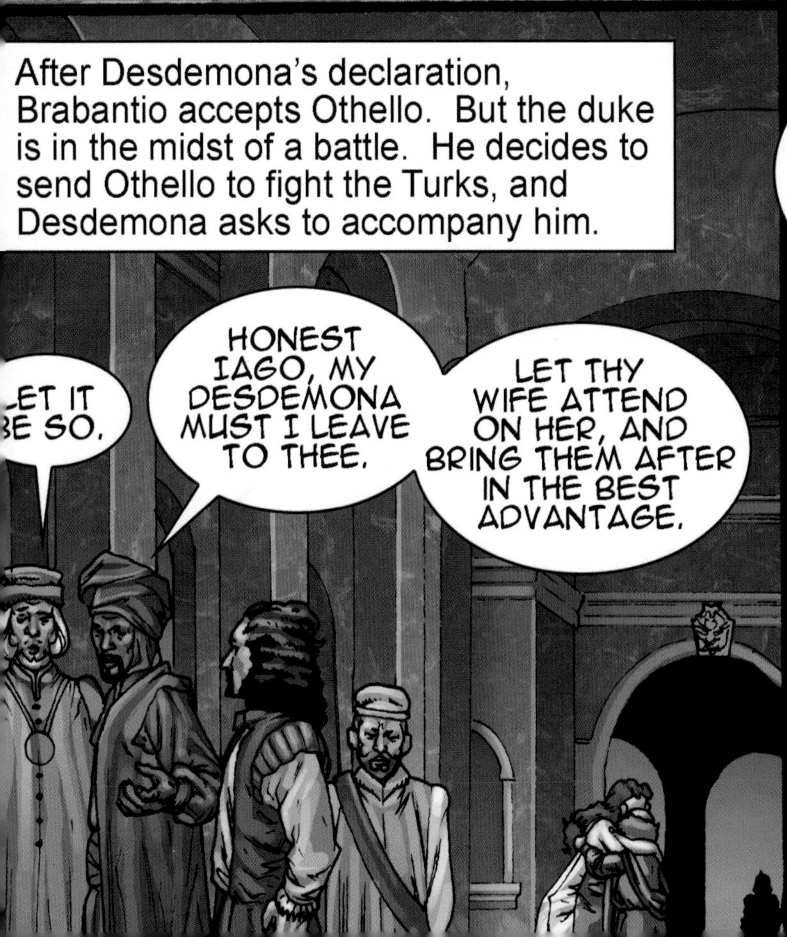
After Desdemona's declaration, Brabantio accepts Othello. But the duke is in the midst of a battle. He decides to send Othello to fight the Turks, and Desdemona asks to accompany him.
LET IT BE SO.
HONEST IAGO, MY DESDEMONA MUST I LEAVE TO THEE.
LET THY WIFE ATTEND ON HER, AND BRING THEM AFTER IN THE BEST ADVANTAGE.

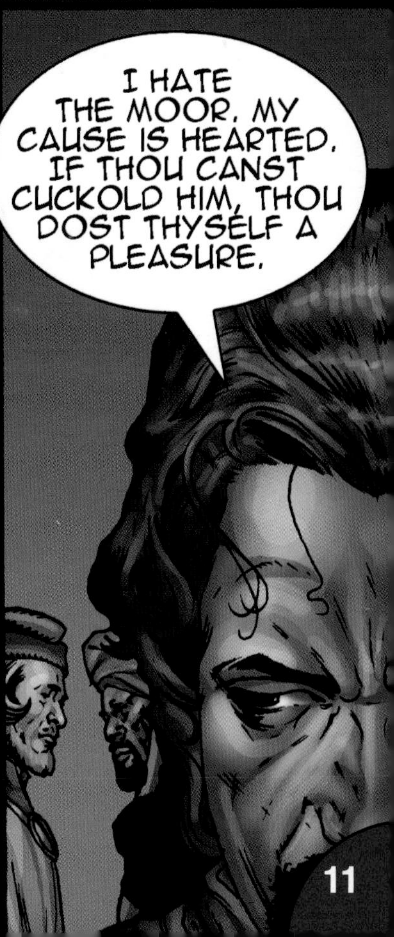
I HATE THE MOOR. MY CAUSE IS HEARTED. IF THOU CANST CUCKOLD HIM, THOU DOST THYSELF A PLEASURE.

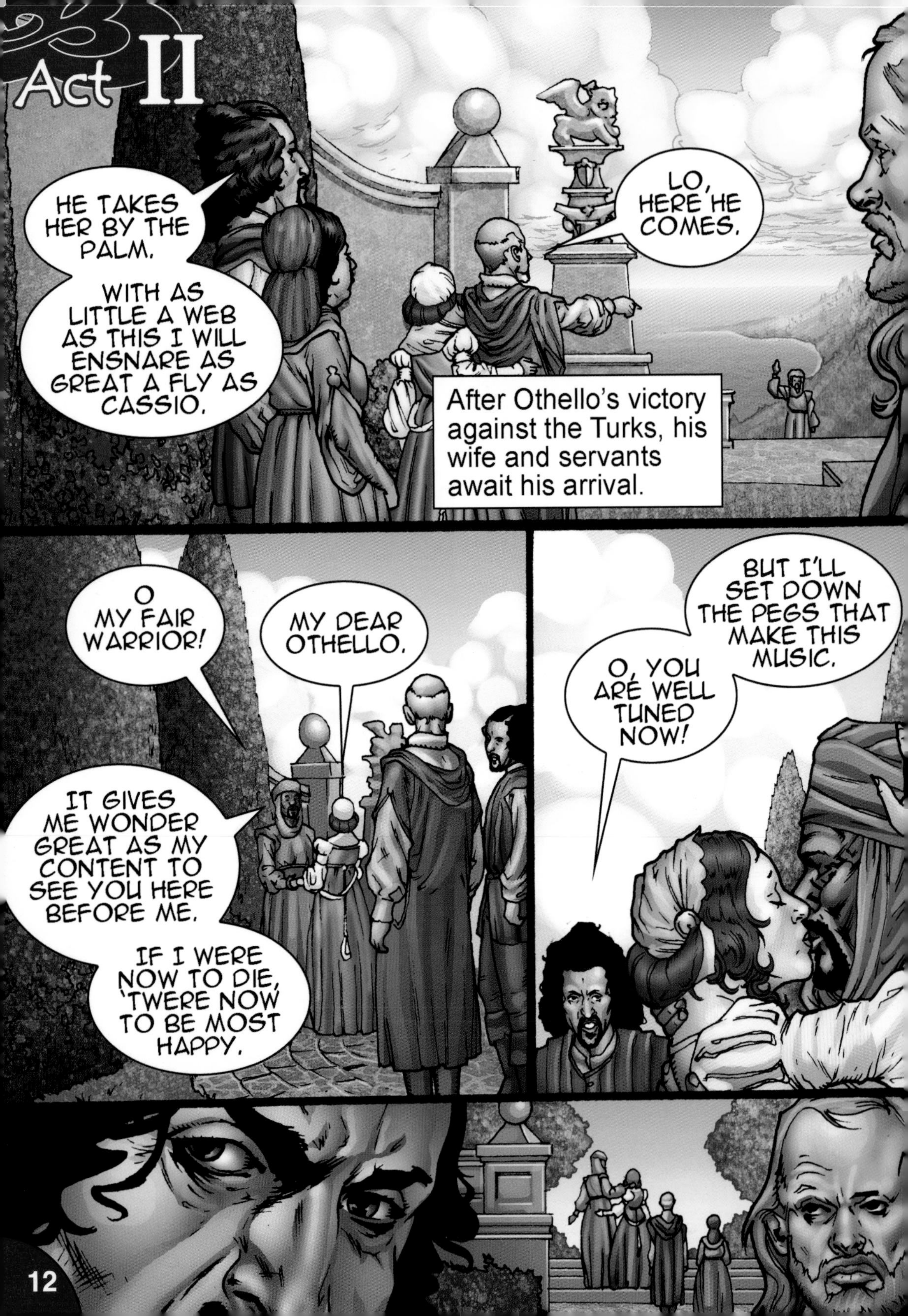
Act II
HE TAKES HER BY THE PALM.
WITH AS LITTLE A WEB AS THIS I WILL ENSNARE AS GREAT A FLY AS CASSIO.
LO, HERE HE COMES.
After Othello's victory against the Turks, his wife and servants await his arrival.
O MY FAIR WARRIOR!
MY DEAR OTHELLO.
IT GIVES ME WONDER GREAT AS MY CONTENT TO SEE YOU HERE BEFORE ME.
IF I WERE NOW TO DIE, 'TWERE NOW TO BE MOST HAPPY.
O, YOU ARE WELL TUNED NOW!
BUT I'LL SET DOWN THE PEGS THAT MAKE THIS MUSIC.

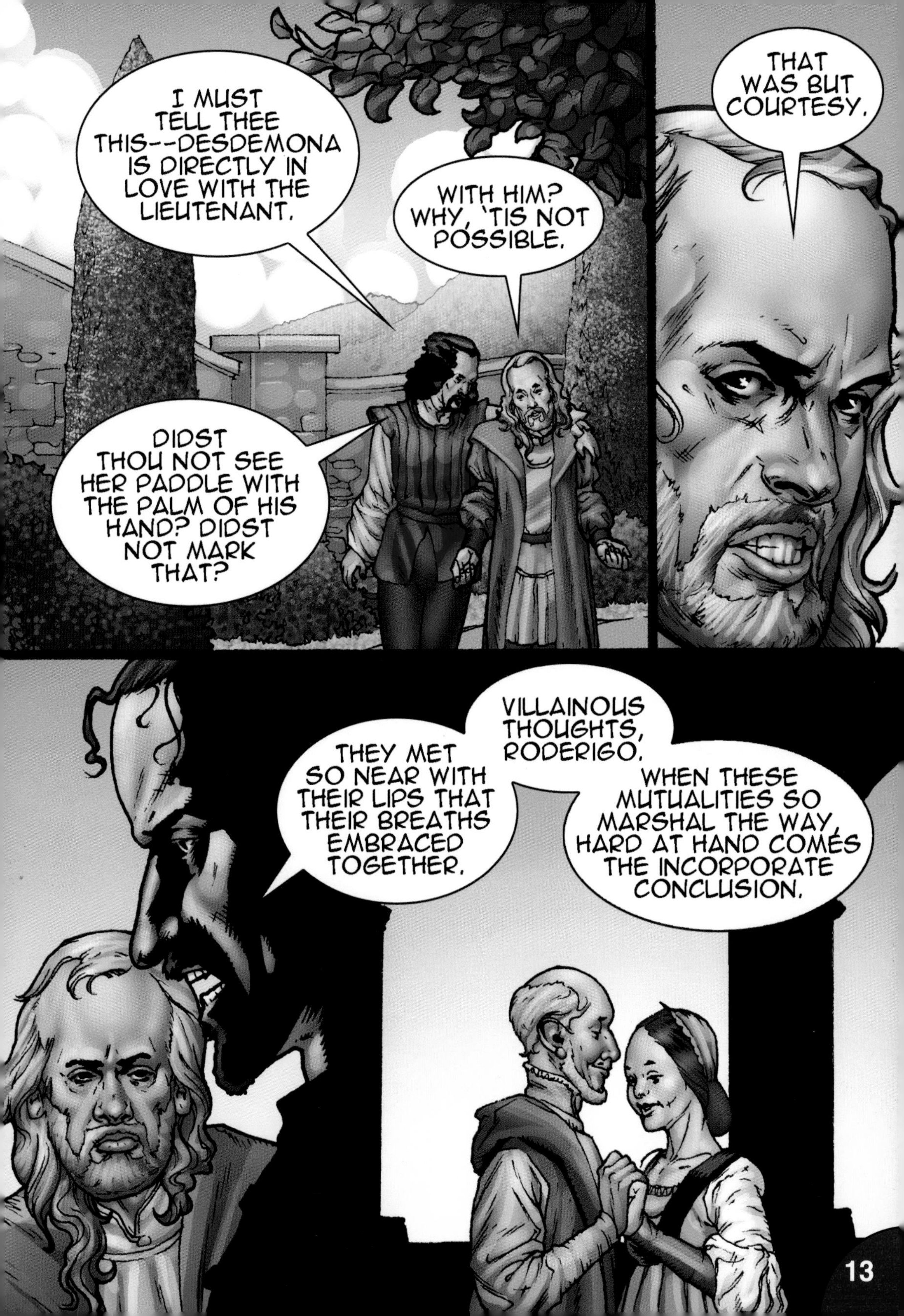
I MUST TELL THEE THIS--DESDEMONA IS DIRECTLY IN LOVE WITH THE LIEUTENANT.
WITH HIM? WHY, 'TIS NOT POSSIBLE.
DIDST THOU NOT SEE HER PADDLE WITH THE PALM OF HIS HAND? DIDST NOT MARK THAT?
THAT WAS BUT COURTESY.
VILLAINOUS THOUGHTS, RODERIGO.
THEY MET SO NEAR WITH THEIR LIPS THAT THEIR BREATHS EMBRACED TOGETHER.
WHEN THESE MUTUALITIES SO MARSHAL THE WAY, HARD AT HAND COMES THE INCORPORATE CONCLUSION.

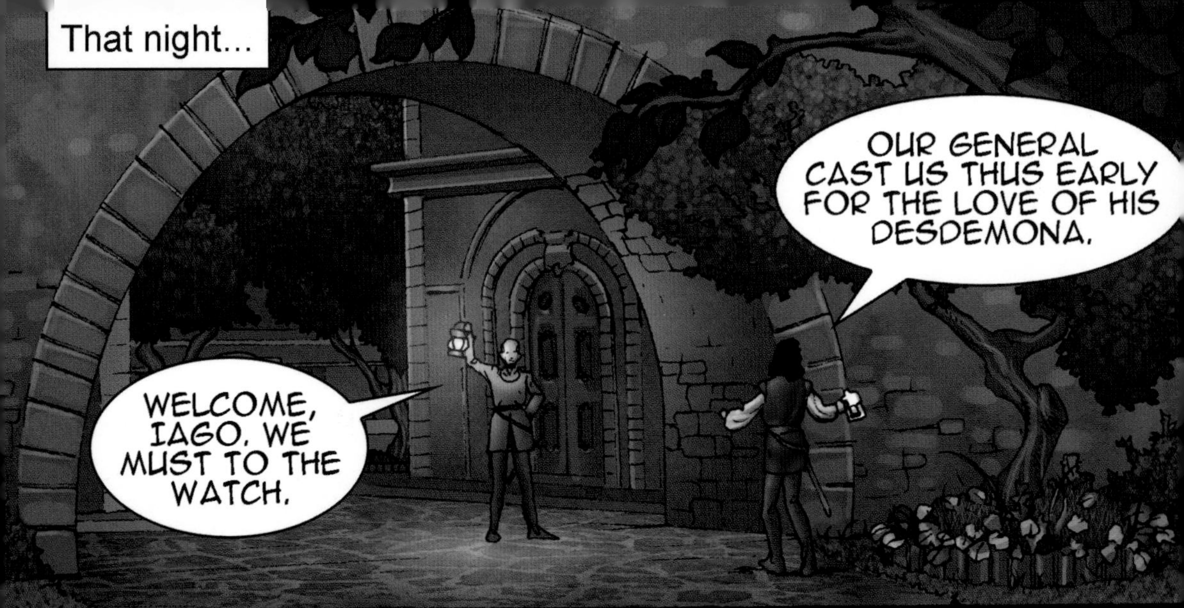
That night...
WELCOME, IAGO. WE MUST TO THE WATCH.
OUR GENERAL CAST US THUS EARLY FOR THE LOVE OF HIS DESDEMONA.

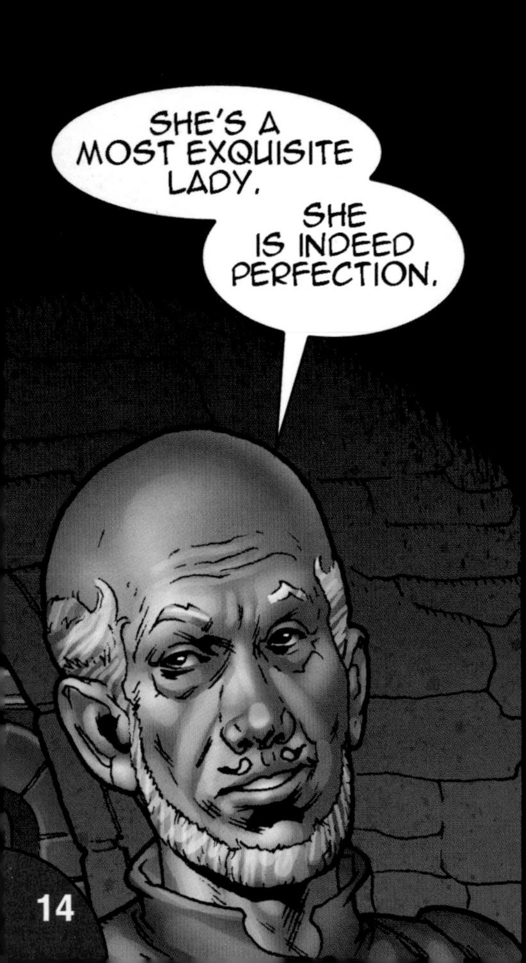
SHE'S A MOST EXQUISITE LADY.
SHE IS INDEED PERFECTION.

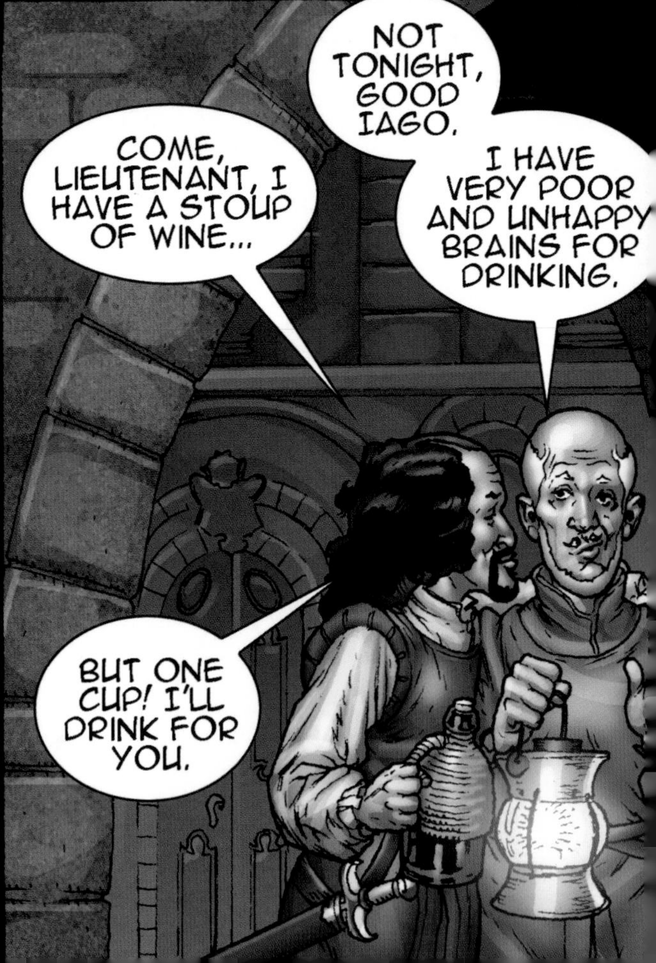
COME, LIEUTENANT, I HAVE A STOUP OF WINE...
NOT TONIGHT, GOOD IAGO.
I HAVE VERY POOR AND UNHAPPY BRAINS FOR DRINKING.
BUT ONE CUP! I'LL DRINK FOR YOU.

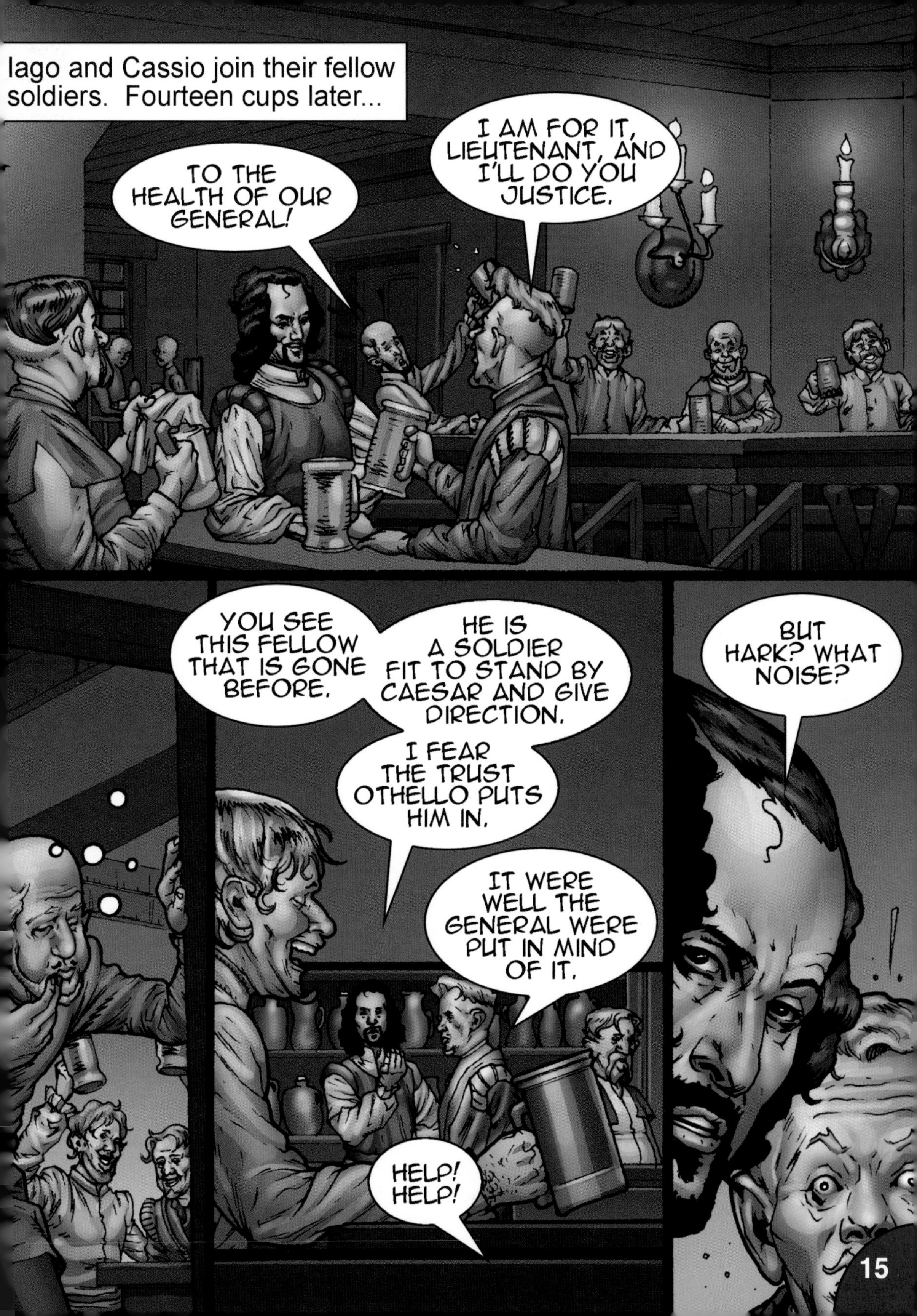
Iago and Cassio join their fellow soldiers. Fourteen cups later...
TO THE HEALTH OF OUR GENERAL!
I AM FOR IT, LIEUTENANT, AND I'LL DO YOU JUSTICE.
YOU SEE THIS FELLOW THAT IS GONE BEFORE.
HE IS A SOLDIER FIT TO STAND BY CAESAR AND GIVE DIRECTION.
I FEAR THE TRUST OTHELLO PUTS HIM IN.
IT WERE WELL THE GENERAL WERE PUT IN MIND OF IT.
HELP! HELP!
BUT HARK? WHAT NOISE?
!

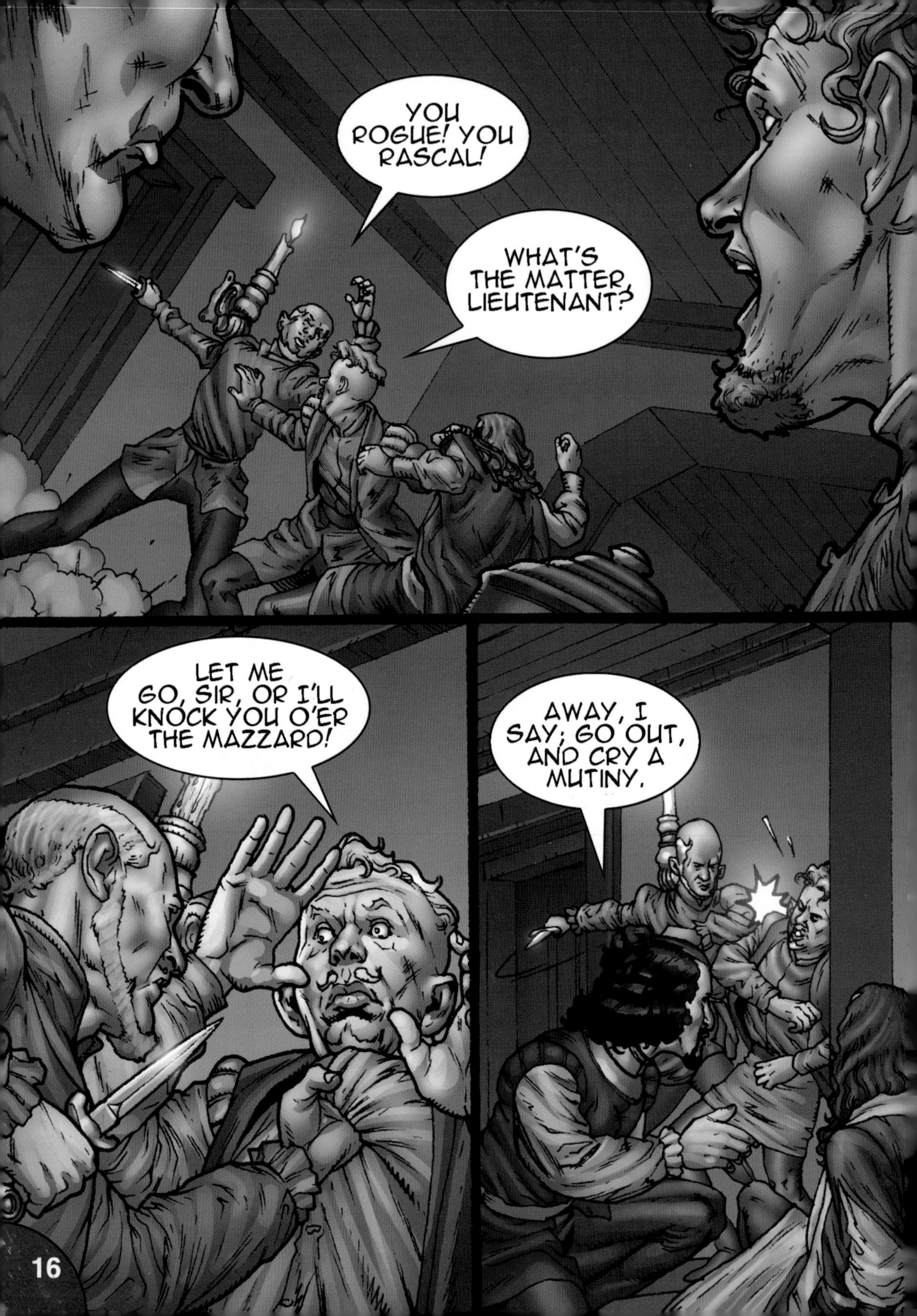
YOU ROGUE! YOU RASCAL!
WHAT'S THE MATTER, LIEUTENANT?
LET ME GO, SIR, OR I'LL KNOCK YOU O'ER THE MAZZARD!
AWAY, I SAY; GO OUT, AND CRY A MUTINY.

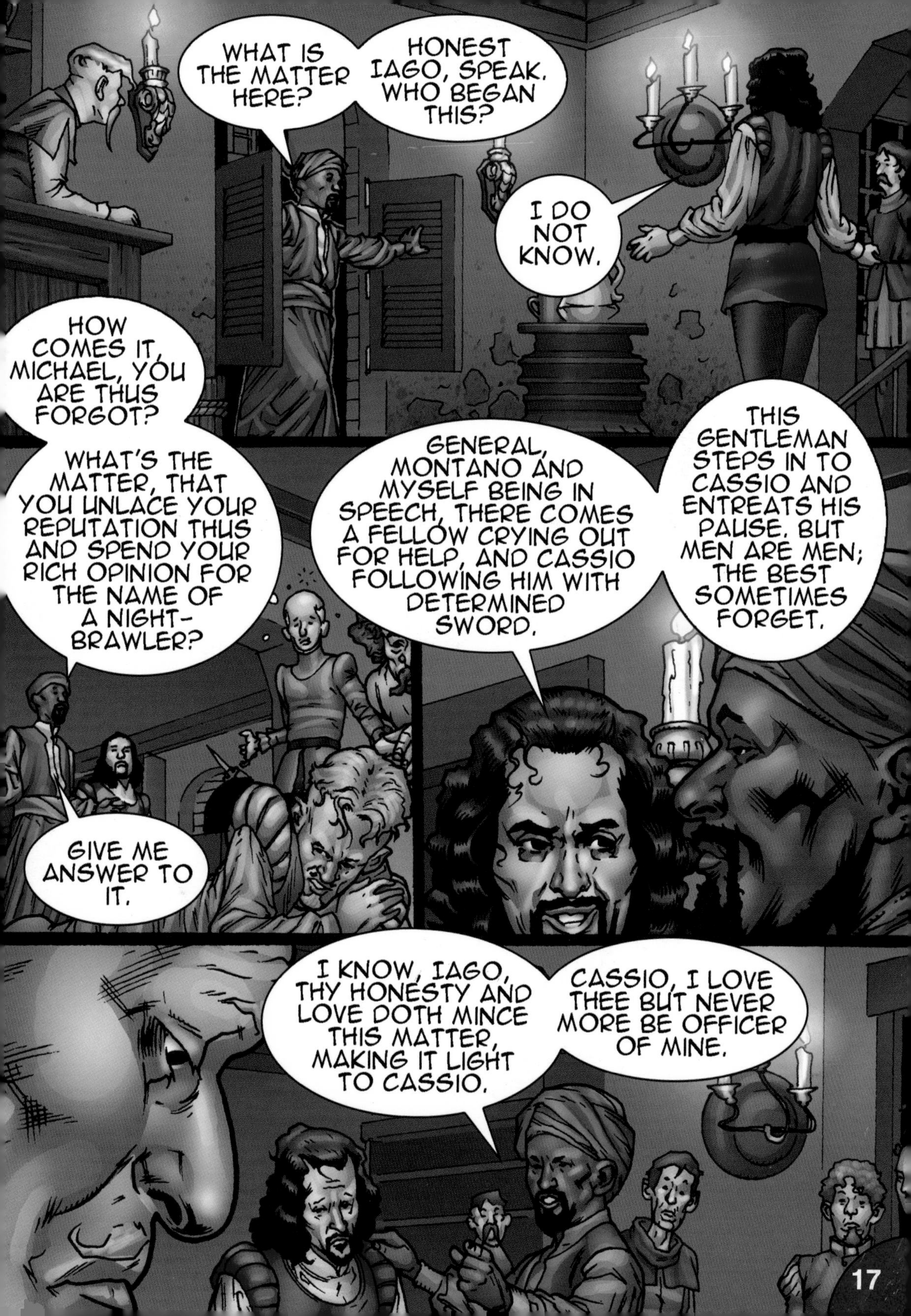
WHAT IS THE MATTER HERE?
HONEST IAGO, SPEAK. WHO BEGAN THIS?
I DO NOT KNOW.
HOW COMES IT, MICHAEL, YOU ARE THUS FORGOT?
WHAT'S THE MATTER, THAT YOU UNLACE YOUR REPUTATION THUS AND SPEND YOUR RICH OPINION FOR THE NAME OF A NIGHT-BRAWLER?
GIVE ME ANSWER TO IT.
GENERAL, MONTANO AND MYSELF BEING IN SPEECH, THERE COMES A FELLOW CRYING OUT FOR HELP, AND CASSIO FOLLOWING HIM WITH DETERMINED SWORD.
THIS GENTLEMAN STEPS IN TO CASSIO AND ENTREATS HIS PAUSE. BUT MEN ARE MEN; THE BEST SOMETIMES FORGET.
I KNOW, IAGO, THY HONESTY AND LOVE DOTH MINCE THIS MATTER, MAKING IT LIGHT TO CASSIO.
CASSIO, I LOVE THEE BUT NEVER MORE BE OFFICER OF MINE.

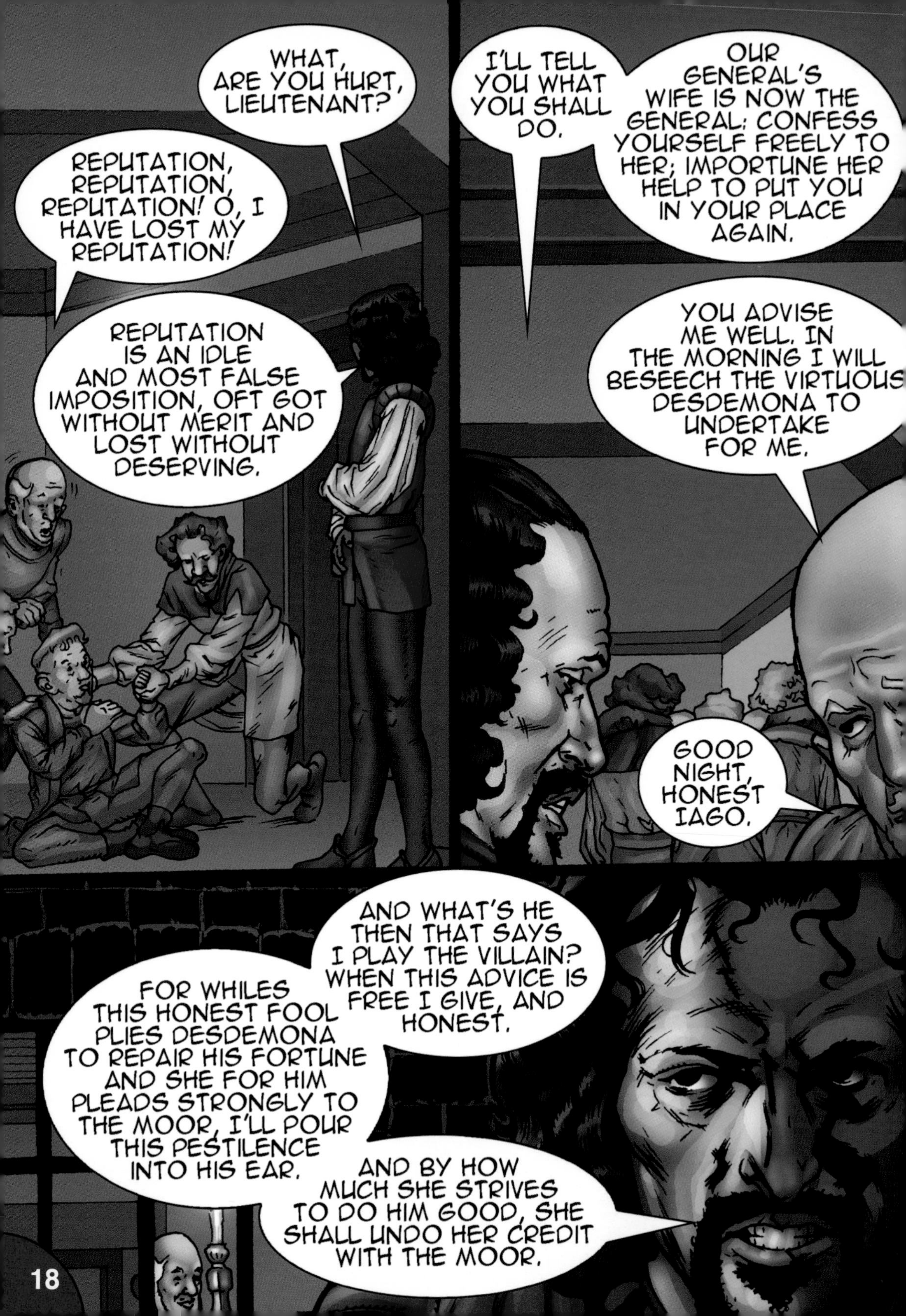
WHAT, ARE YOU HURT, LIEUTENANT?
REPUTATION, REPUTATION, REPUTATION! O, I HAVE LOST MY REPUTATION!
REPUTATION IS AN IDLE AND MOST FALSE IMPOSITION, OFT GOT WITHOUT MERIT AND LOST WITHOUT DESERVING.
I'LL TELL YOU WHAT YOU SHALL DO.
OUR GENERAL'S WIFE IS NOW THE GENERAL: CONFESS YOURSELF FREELY TO HER; IMPORTUNE HER HELP TO PUT YOU IN YOUR PLACE AGAIN.
YOU ADVISE ME WELL. IN THE MORNING I WILL BESEECH THE VIRTUOUS DESDEMONA TO UNDERTAKE FOR ME.
GOOD NIGHT, HONEST IAGO.
AND WHAT'S HE THEN THAT SAYS I PLAY THE VILLAIN? WHEN THIS ADVICE IS FREE I GIVE, AND HONEST.
FOR WHILES THIS HONEST FOOL PLIES DESDEMONA TO REPAIR HIS FORTUNE AND SHE FOR HIM PLEADS STRONGLY TO THE MOOR, I'LL POUR THIS PESTILENCE INTO HIS EAR.
AND BY HOW MUCH SHE STRIVES TO DO HIM GOOD, SHE SHALL UNDO HER CREDIT WITH THE MOOR.

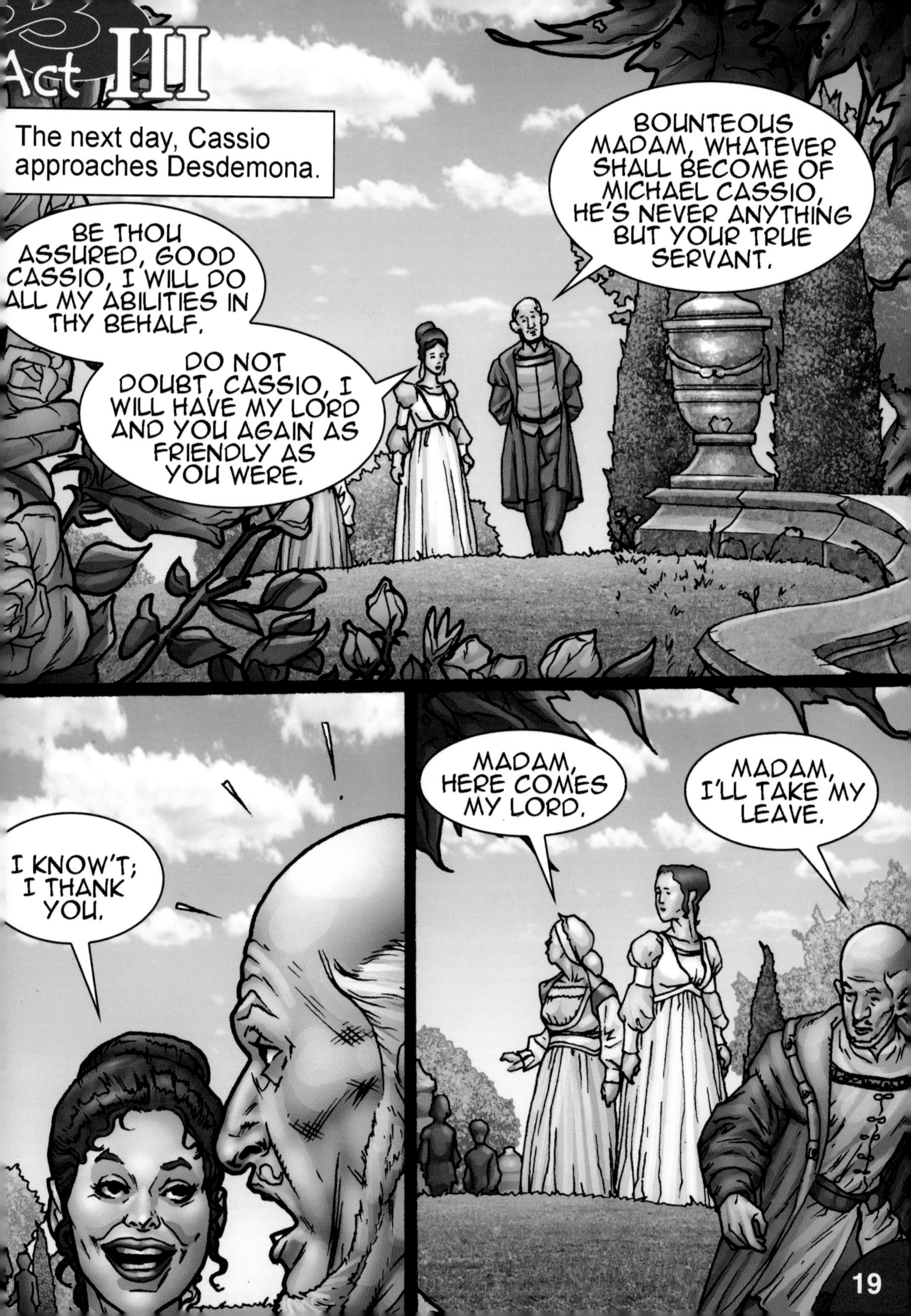
Act III
The next day, Cassio approaches Desdemona.
BOUNTEOUS MADAM, WHATEVER SHALL BECOME OF MICHAEL CASSIO, HE'S NEVER ANYTHING BUT YOUR TRUE SERVANT.
BE THOU ASSURED, GOOD CASSIO, I WILL DO ALL MY ABILITIES IN THY BEHALF.
DO NOT DOUBT, CASSIO, I WILL HAVE MY LORD AND YOU AGAIN AS FRIENDLY AS YOU WERE.
I KNOW'T; I THANK YOU.
MADAM, HERE COMES MY LORD.
MADAM, I'LL TAKE MY LEAVE.

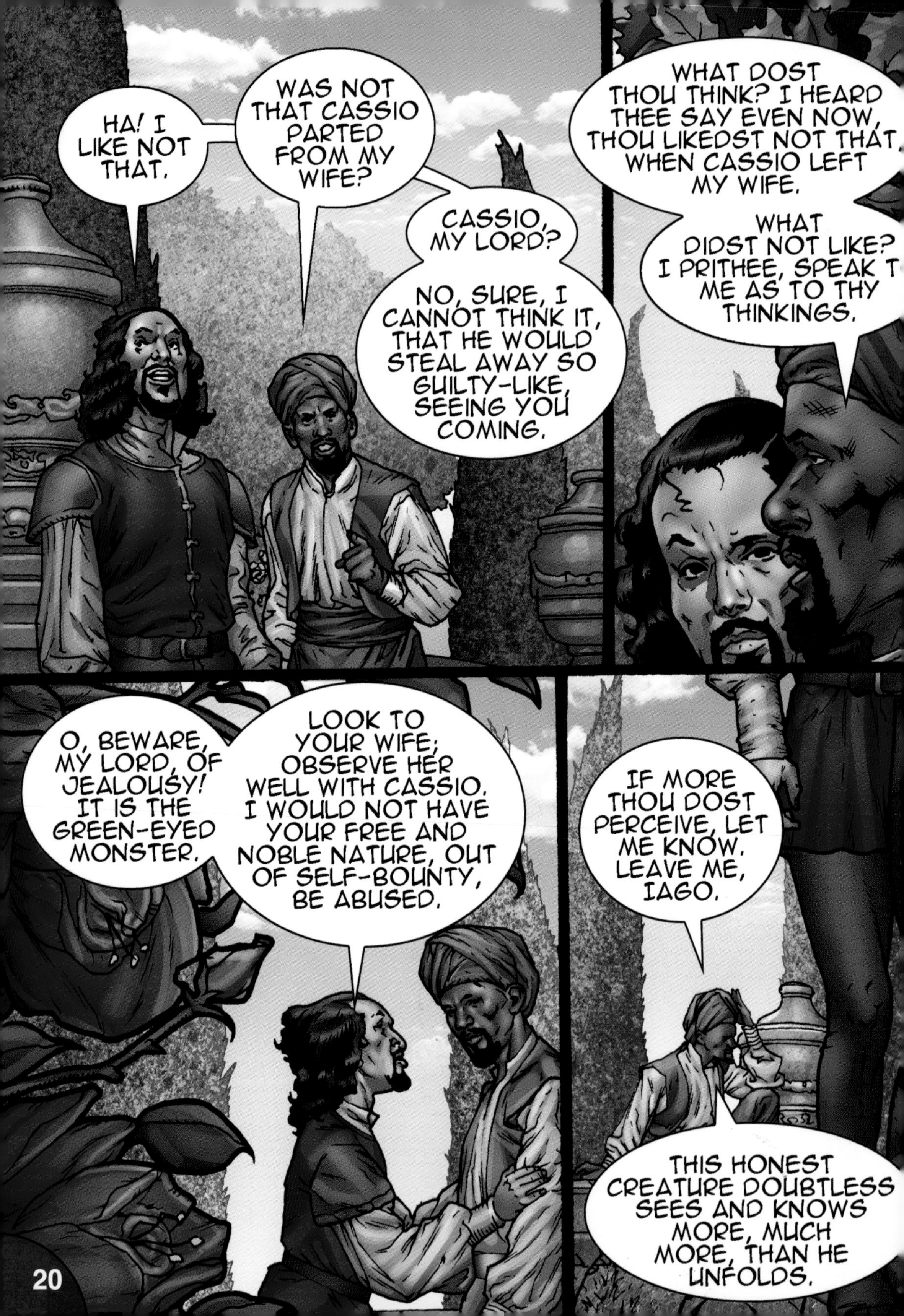
HA! I LIKE NOT THAT.
WAS NOT THAT CASSIO PARTED FROM MY WIFE?
CASSIO, MY LORD?
NO, SURE, I CANNOT THINK IT, THAT HE WOULD STEAL AWAY SO GUILTY-LIKE, SEEING YOU COMING.
WHAT DOST THOU THINK? I HEARD THEE SAY EVEN NOW, THOU LIKEDST NOT THAT, WHEN CASSIO LEFT MY WIFE.
WHAT DIDST NOT LIKE? I PRITHEE, SPEAK T ME AS TO THY THINKINGS.
O, BEWARE, MY LORD, OF JEALOUSY! IT IS THE GREEN-EYED MONSTER.
LOOK TO YOUR WIFE; OBSERVE HER WELL WITH CASSIO. I WOULD NOT HAVE YOUR FREE AND NOBLE NATURE, OUT OF SELF-BOUNTY, BE ABUSED.
IF MORE THOU DOST PERCEIVE, LET ME KNOW. LEAVE ME, IAGO.
THIS HONEST CREATURE DOUBTLESS SEES AND KNOWS MORE, MUCH MORE, THAN HE UNFOLDS.

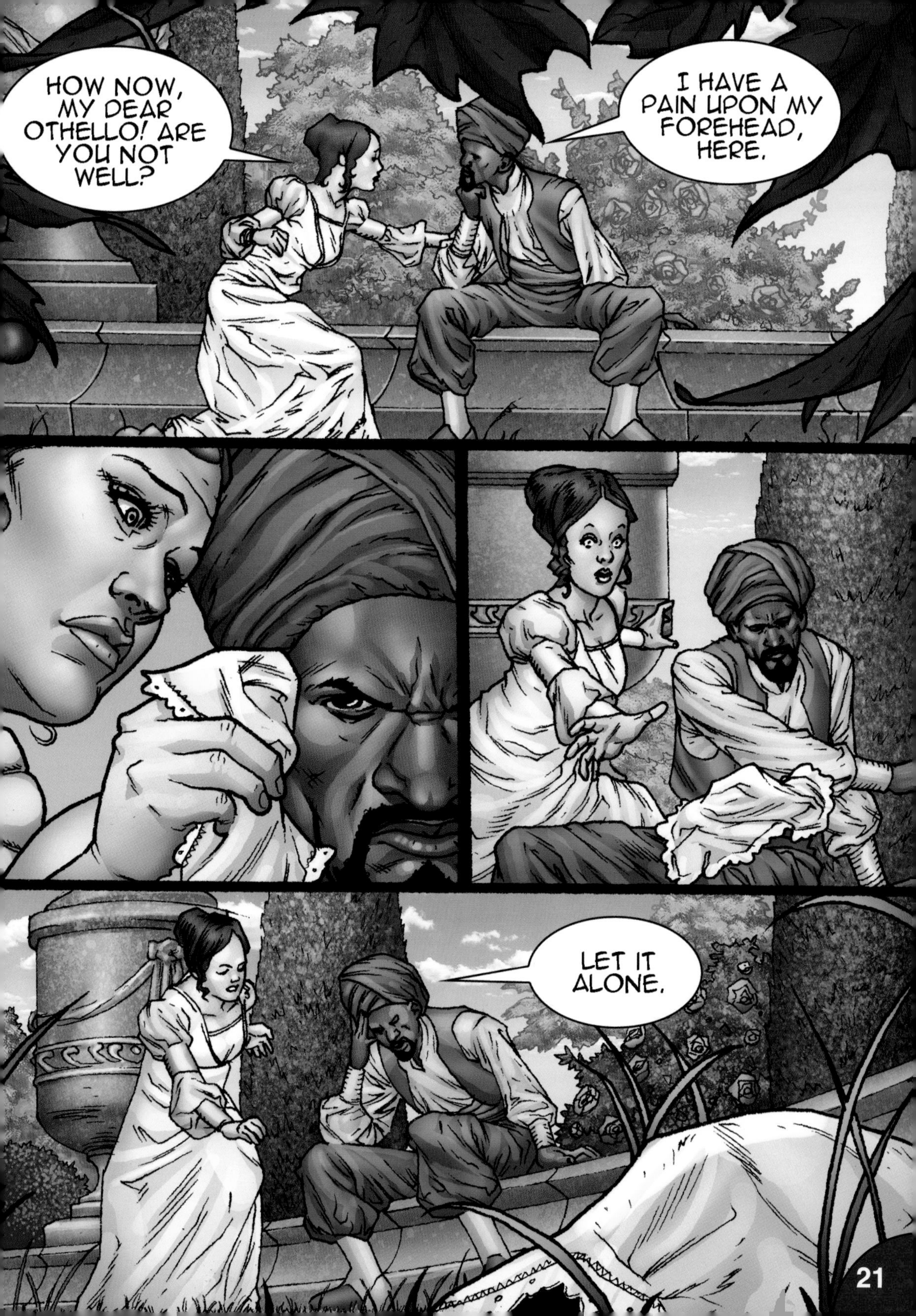
HOW NOW, MY DEAR OTHELLO! ARE YOU NOT WELL?
I HAVE A PAIN UPON MY FOREHEAD, HERE.
LET IT ALONE.

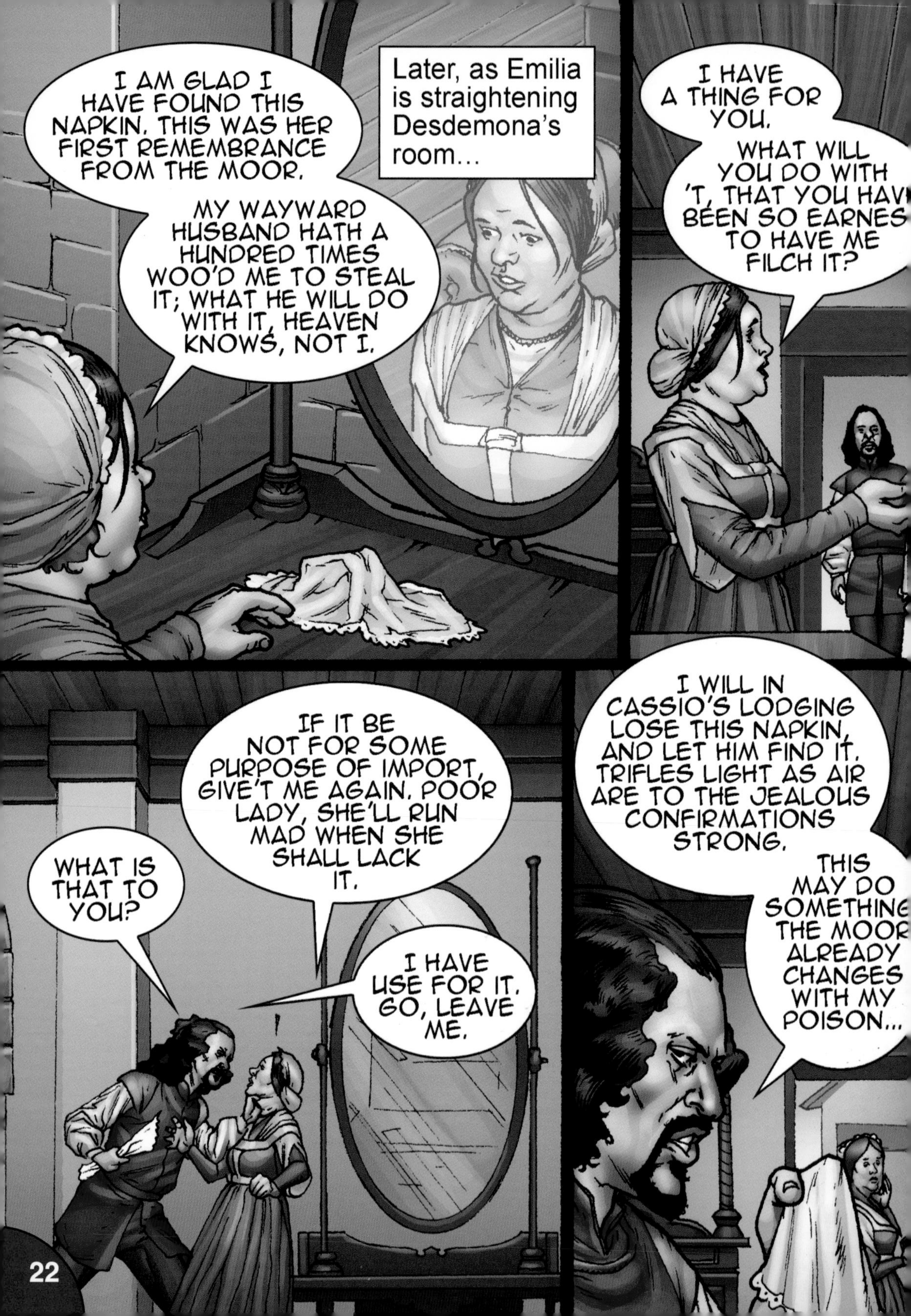

I AM GLAD I HAVE FOUND THIS NAPKIN. THIS WAS HER FIRST REMEMBRANCE FROM THE MOOR.
MY WAYWARD HUSBAND HATH A HUNDRED TIMES WOO'D ME TO STEAL IT; WHAT HE WILL DO WITH IT, HEAVEN KNOWS, NOT I.
Later, as Emilia is straightening Desdemona's room…
I HAVE A THING FOR YOU.
WHAT WILL YOU DO WITH 'T, THAT YOU HAV BEEN SO EARNES TO HAVE ME FILCH IT?
WHAT IS THAT TO YOU?
IF IT BE NOT FOR SOME PURPOSE OF IMPORT, GIVE'T ME AGAIN. POOR LADY, SHE'LL RUN MAD WHEN SHE SHALL LACK IT.
I HAVE USE FOR IT. GO, LEAVE ME.
!
I WILL IN CASSIO'S LODGING LOSE THIS NAPKIN, AND LET HIM FIND IT. TRIFLES LIGHT AS AIR ARE TO THE JEALOUS CONFIRMATIONS STRONG.
THIS MAY DO SOMETHING THE MOOR ALREADY CHANGES WITH MY POISON...

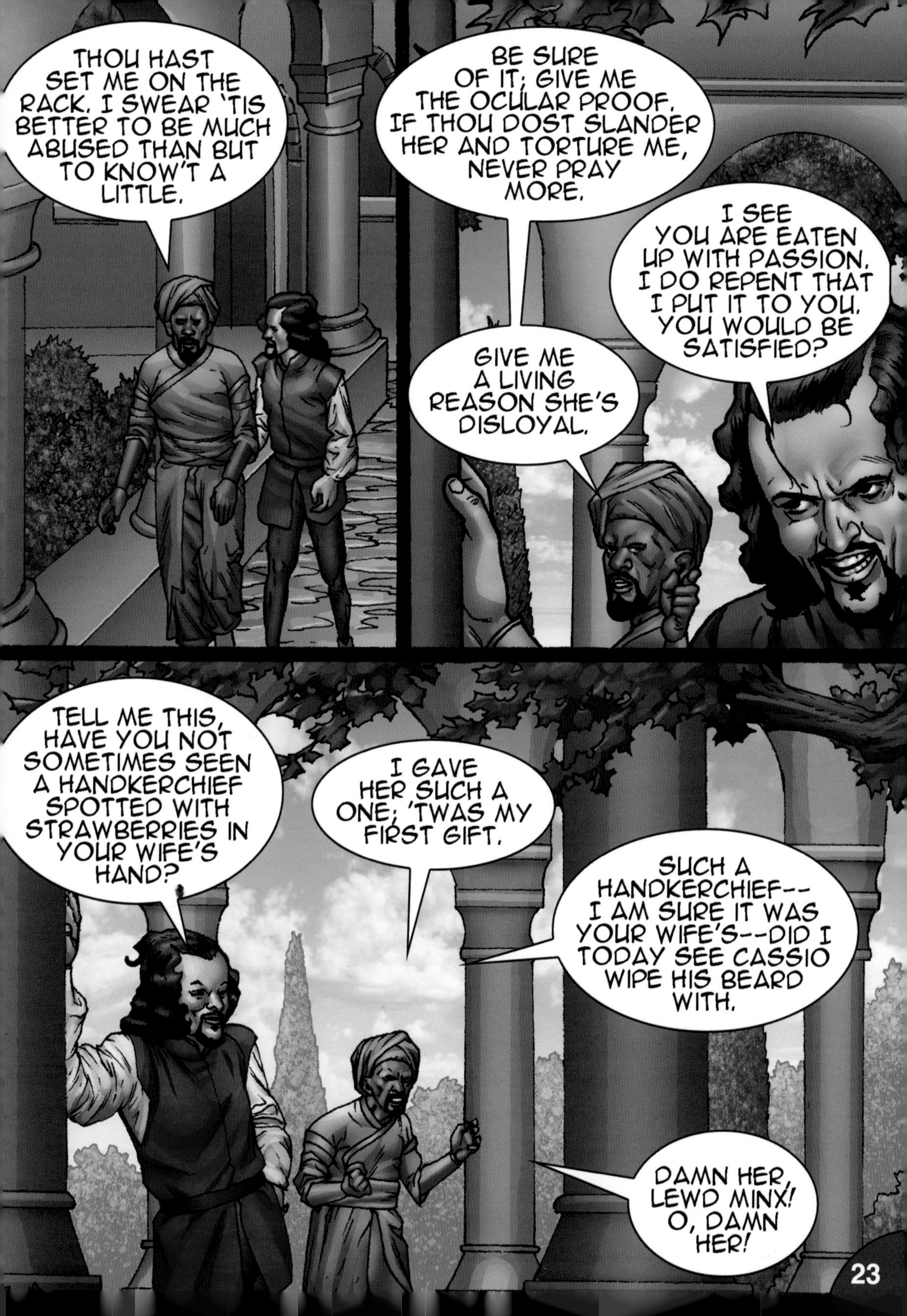
THOU HAST SET ME ON THE RACK. I SWEAR 'TIS BETTER TO BE MUCH ABUSED THAN BUT TO KNOW'T A LITTLE.
BE SURE OF IT; GIVE ME THE OCULAR PROOF. IF THOU DOST SLANDER HER AND TORTURE ME, NEVER PRAY MORE.
I SEE YOU ARE EATEN UP WITH PASSION. I DO REPENT THAT I PUT IT TO YOU. YOU WOULD BE SATISFIED?
GIVE ME A LIVING REASON SHE'S DISLOYAL.
TELL ME THIS, HAVE YOU NOT SOMETIMES SEEN A HANDKERCHIEF SPOTTED WITH STRAWBERRIES IN YOUR WIFE'S HAND?
I GAVE HER SUCH A ONE; 'TWAS MY FIRST GIFT.
SUCH A HANDKERCHIEF-- I AM SURE IT WAS YOUR WIFE'S--DID I TODAY SEE CASSIO WIPE HIS BEARD WITH.
DAMN HER, LEWD MINX! O, DAMN HER!

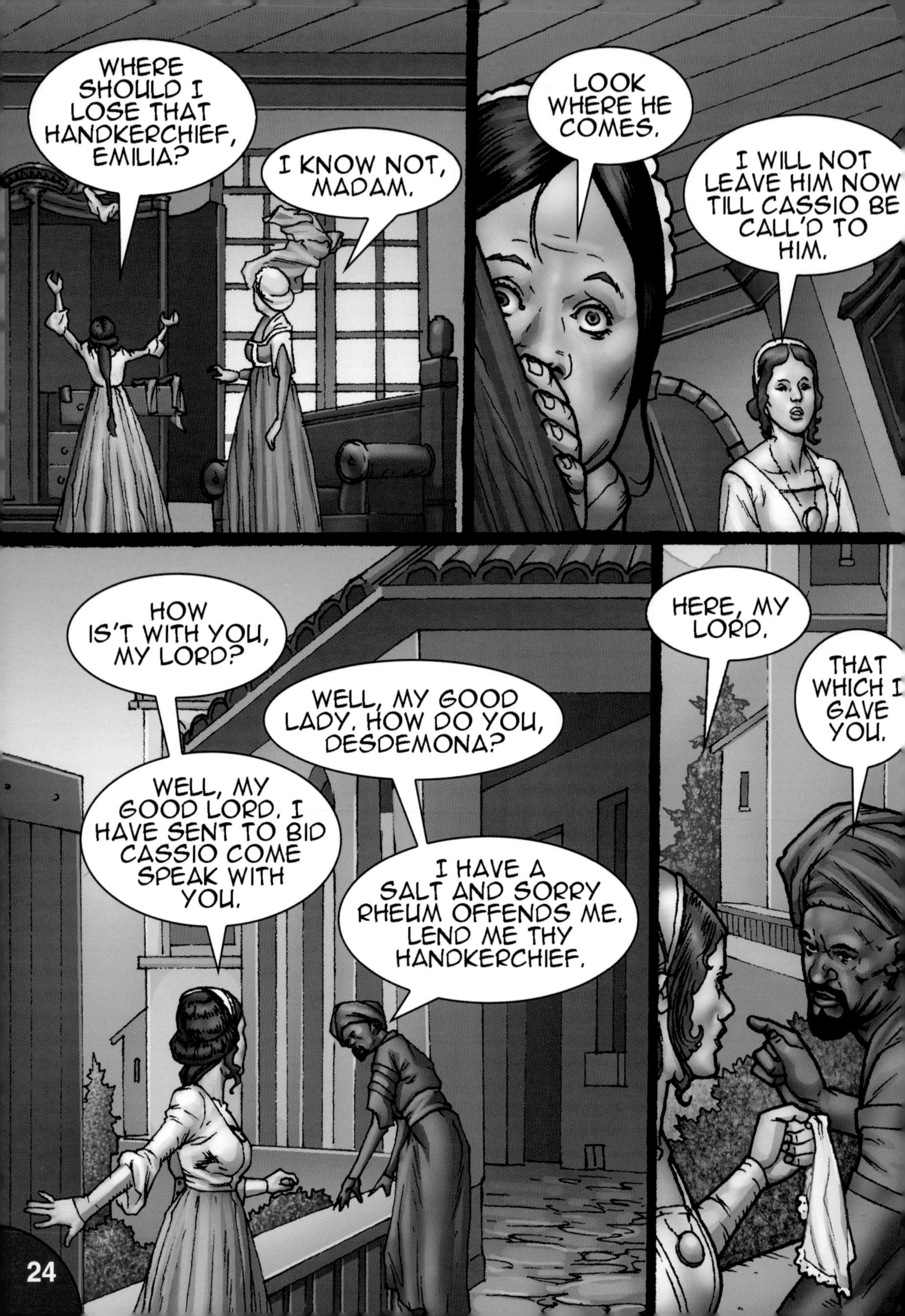
WHERE SHOULD I LOSE THAT HANDKERCHIEF, EMILIA?
I KNOW NOT, MADAM.
LOOK WHERE HE COMES.
I WILL NOT LEAVE HIM NOW TILL CASSIO BE CALL'D TO HIM.
HOW IS'T WITH YOU, MY LORD?
WELL, MY GOOD LADY. HOW DO YOU, DESDEMONA?
WELL, MY GOOD LORD. I HAVE SENT TO BID CASSIO COME SPEAK WITH YOU.
I HAVE A SALT AND SORRY RHEUM OFFENDS ME. LEND ME THY HANDKERCHIEF.
HERE, MY LORD.
THAT WHICH I GAVE YOU.

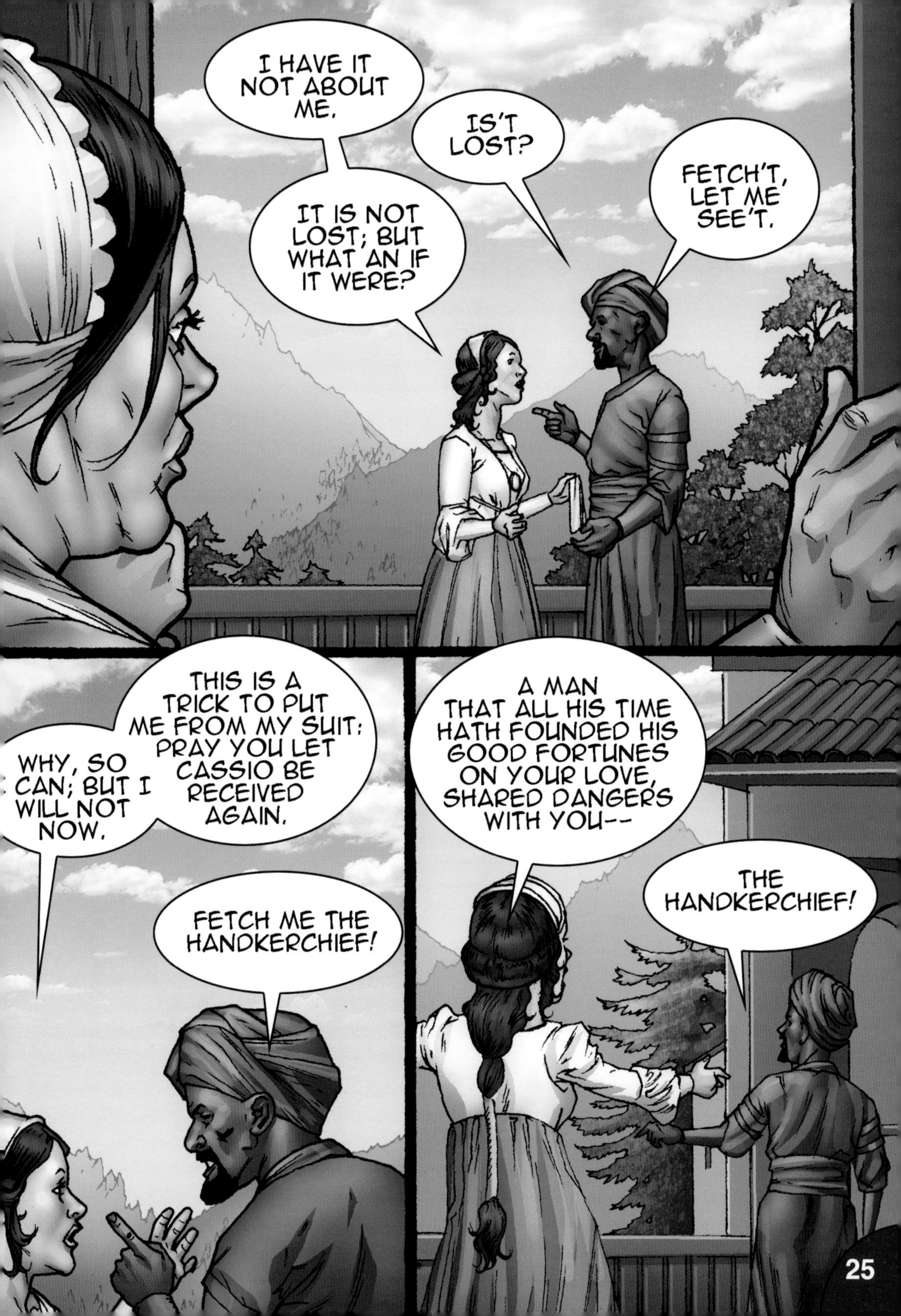
I HAVE IT NOT ABOUT ME.
IS'T LOST?
IT IS NOT LOST; BUT WHAT AN IF IT WERE?
FETCH'T, LET ME SEE'T.
WHY, SO CAN; BUT I WILL NOT NOW.
THIS IS A TRICK TO PUT ME FROM MY SUIT: PRAY YOU LET CASSIO BE RECEIVED AGAIN.
FETCH ME THE HANDKERCHIEF!
A MAN THAT ALL HIS TIME HATH FOUNDED HIS GOOD FORTUNES ON YOUR LOVE, SHARED DANGERS WITH YOU--
THE HANDKERCHIEF!

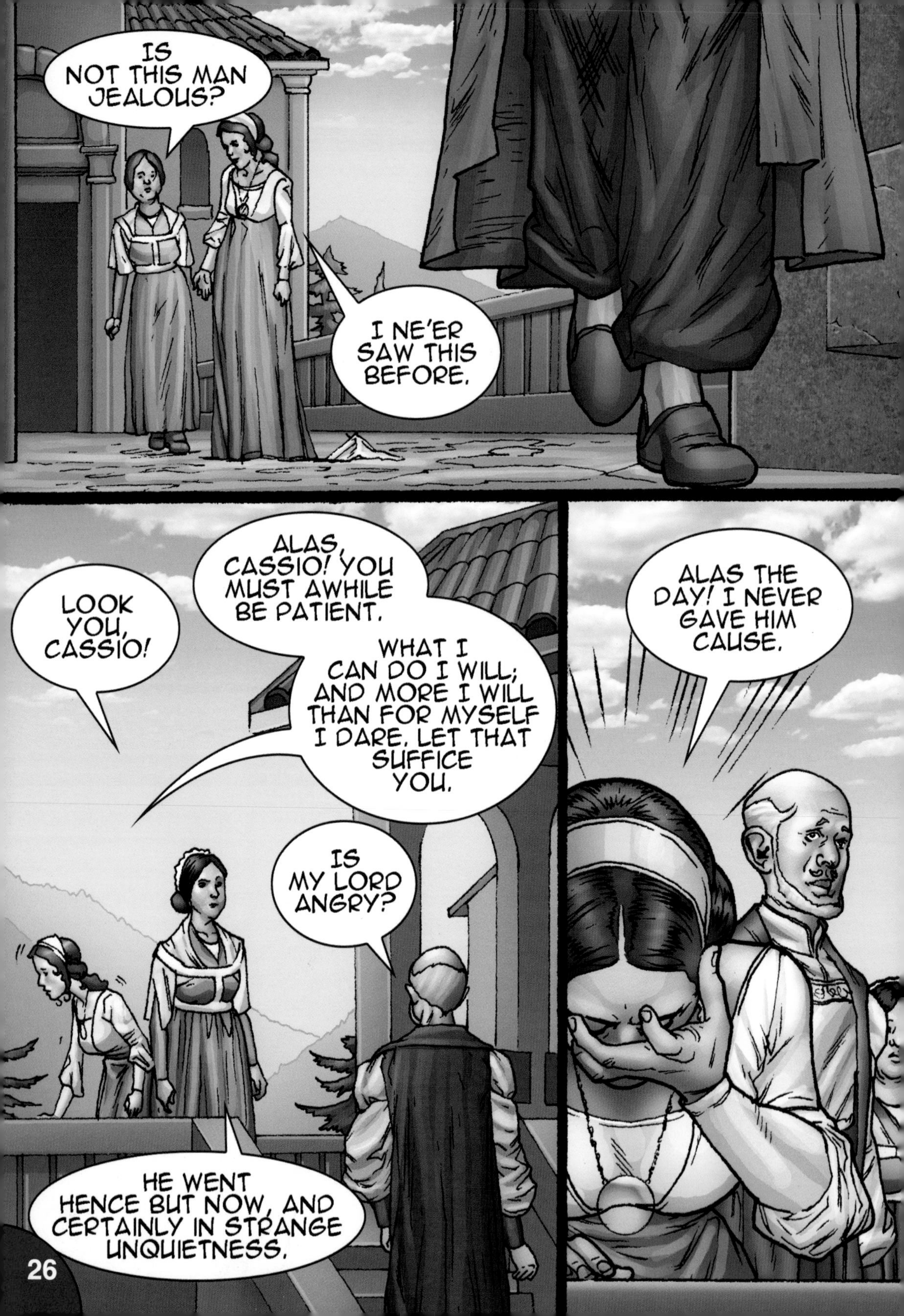
IS NOT THIS MAN JEALOUS?
I NE'ER SAW THIS BEFORE.
LOOK YOU, CASSIO!
ALAS, CASSIO! YOU MUST AWHILE BE PATIENT.
WHAT I CAN DO I WILL; AND MORE I WILL THAN FOR MYSELF I DARE. LET THAT SUFFICE YOU.
IS MY LORD ANGRY?
HE WENT HENCE BUT NOW, AND CERTAINLY IN STRANGE UNQUIETNESS.
ALAS THE DAY! I NEVER GAVE HIM CAUSE.

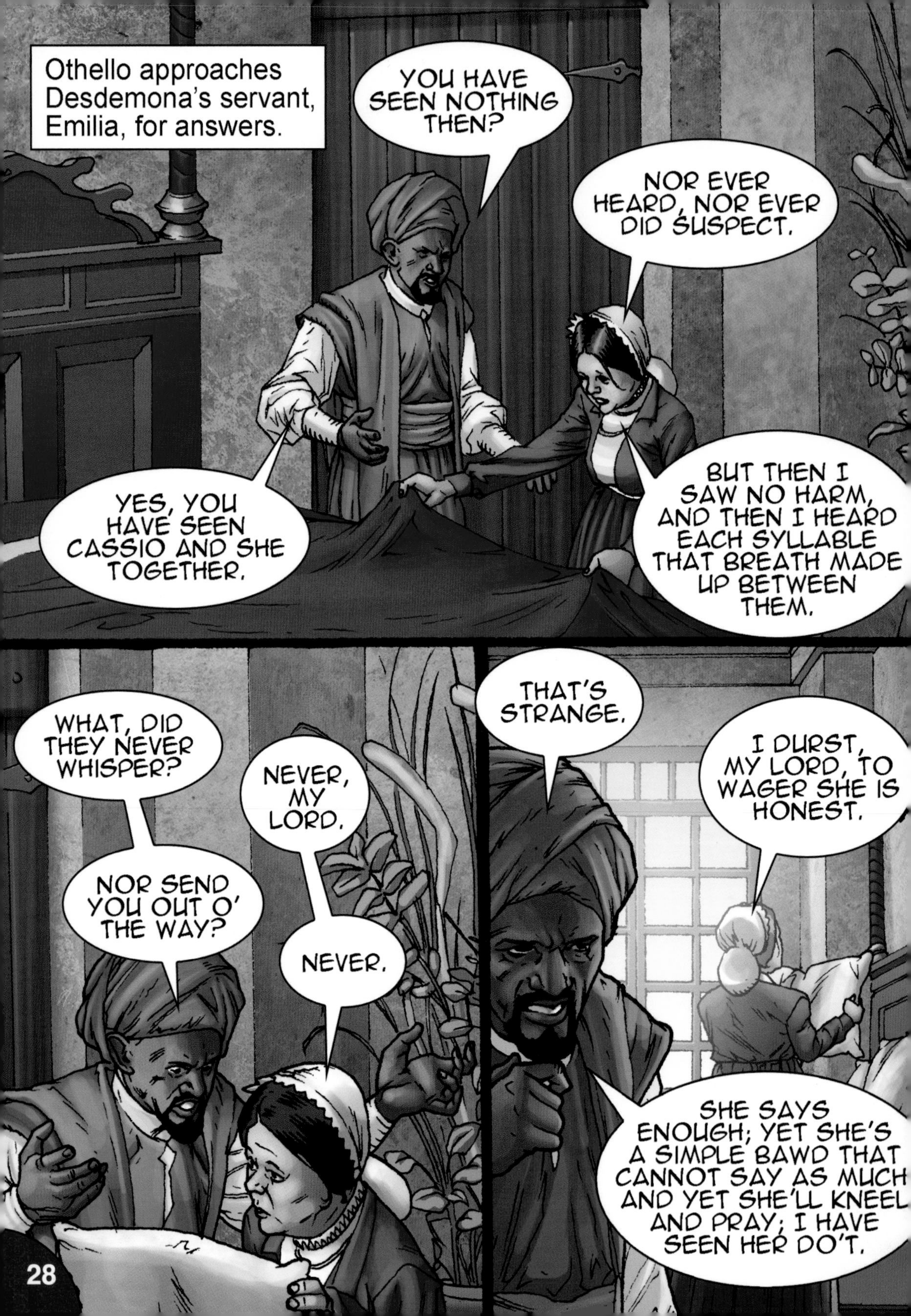
Othello approaches Desdemona's servant, Emilia, for answers.
YOU HAVE SEEN NOTHING THEN?
NOR EVER HEARD, NOR EVER DID SUSPECT.
YES, YOU HAVE SEEN CASSIO AND SHE TOGETHER.
BUT THEN I SAW NO HARM, AND THEN I HEARD EACH SYLLABLE THAT BREATH MADE UP BETWEEN THEM.
WHAT, DID THEY NEVER WHISPER?
NEVER, MY LORD.
NOR SEND YOU OUT O' THE WAY?
NEVER.
THAT'S STRANGE.
I DURST, MY LORD, TO WAGER SHE IS HONEST.
SHE SAYS ENOUGH; YET SHE'S A SIMPLE BAWD THAT CANNOT SAY AS MUCH AND YET SHE'LL KNEEL AND PRAY; I HAVE SEEN HER DO'T.

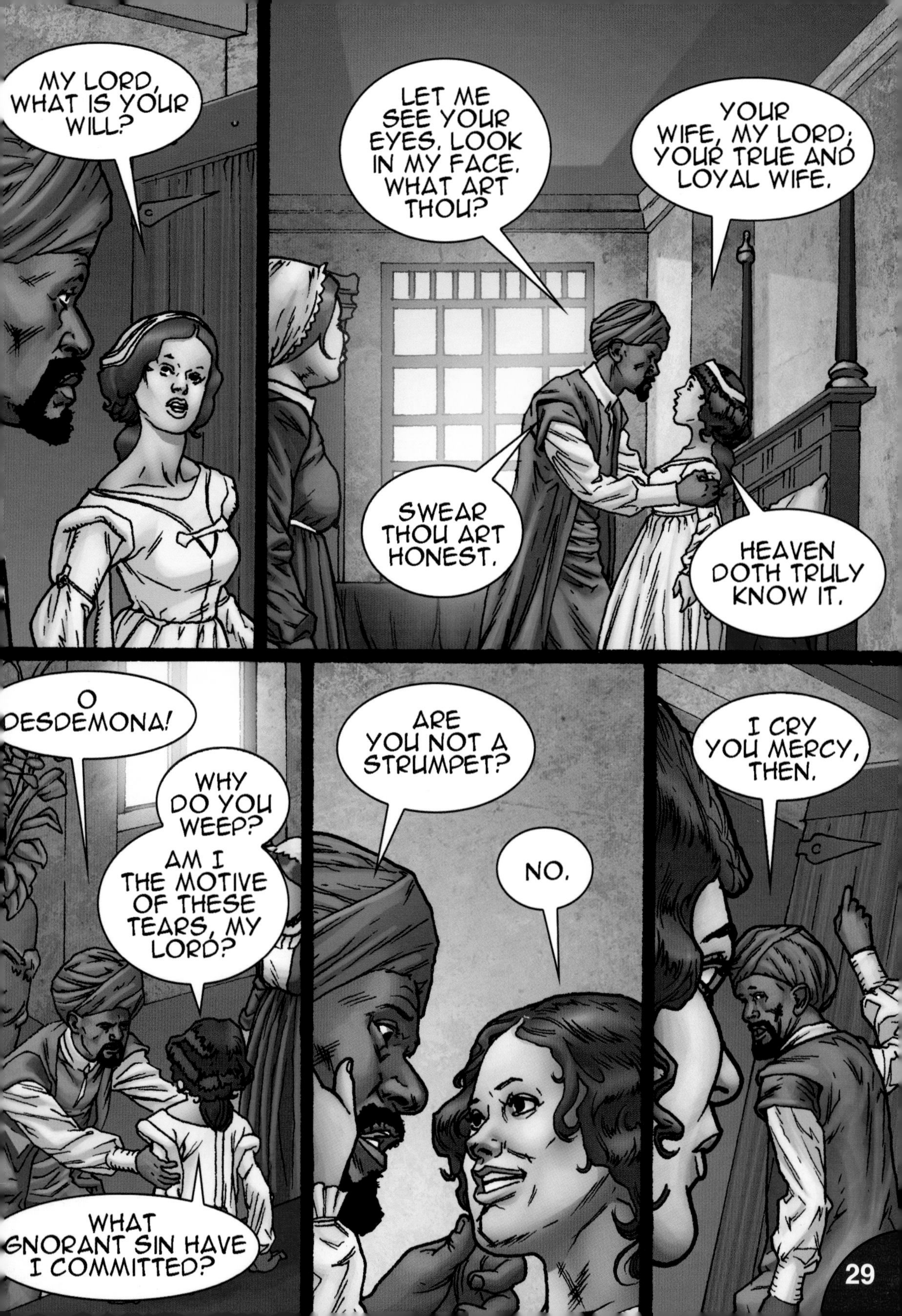
MY LORD, WHAT IS YOUR WILL?
LET ME SEE YOUR EYES. LOOK IN MY FACE. WHAT ART THOU?
YOUR WIFE, MY LORD; YOUR TRUE AND LOYAL WIFE.
SWEAR THOU ART HONEST.
HEAVEN DOTH TRULY KNOW IT.
O DESDEMONA!
WHY DO YOU WEEP?
AM I THE MOTIVE OF THESE TEARS, MY LORD?
WHAT GNORANT SIN HAVE I COMMITTED?
ARE YOU NOT A STRUMPET?
NO.
I CRY YOU MERCY, THEN.

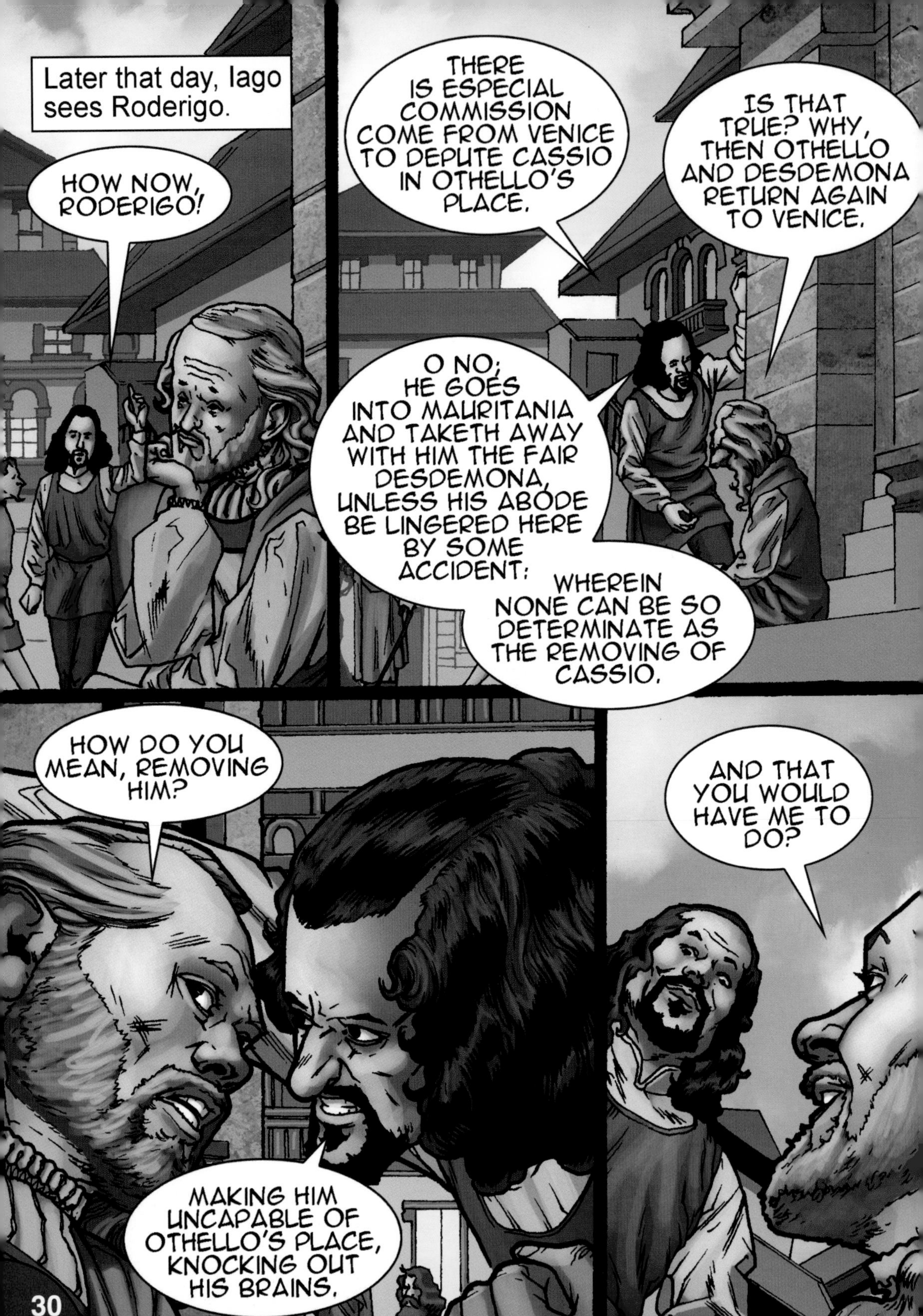
Later that day, Iago sees Roderigo.
HOW NOW, RODERIGO!
THERE IS ESPECIAL COMMISSION COME FROM VENICE TO DEPUTE CASSIO IN OTHELLO'S PLACE.
IS THAT TRUE? WHY, THEN OTHELLO AND DESDEMONA RETURN AGAIN TO VENICE.
O NO; HE GOES INTO MAURITANIA AND TAKETH AWAY WITH HIM THE FAIR DESDEMONA, UNLESS HIS ABODE BE LINGERED HERE BY SOME ACCIDENT:
WHEREIN NONE CAN BE SO DETERMINATE AS THE REMOVING OF CASSIO.
HOW DO YOU MEAN, REMOVING HIM?
MAKING HIM UNCAPABLE OF OTHELLO'S PLACE, KNOCKING OUT HIS BRAINS.
AND THAT YOU WOULD HAVE ME TO DO?

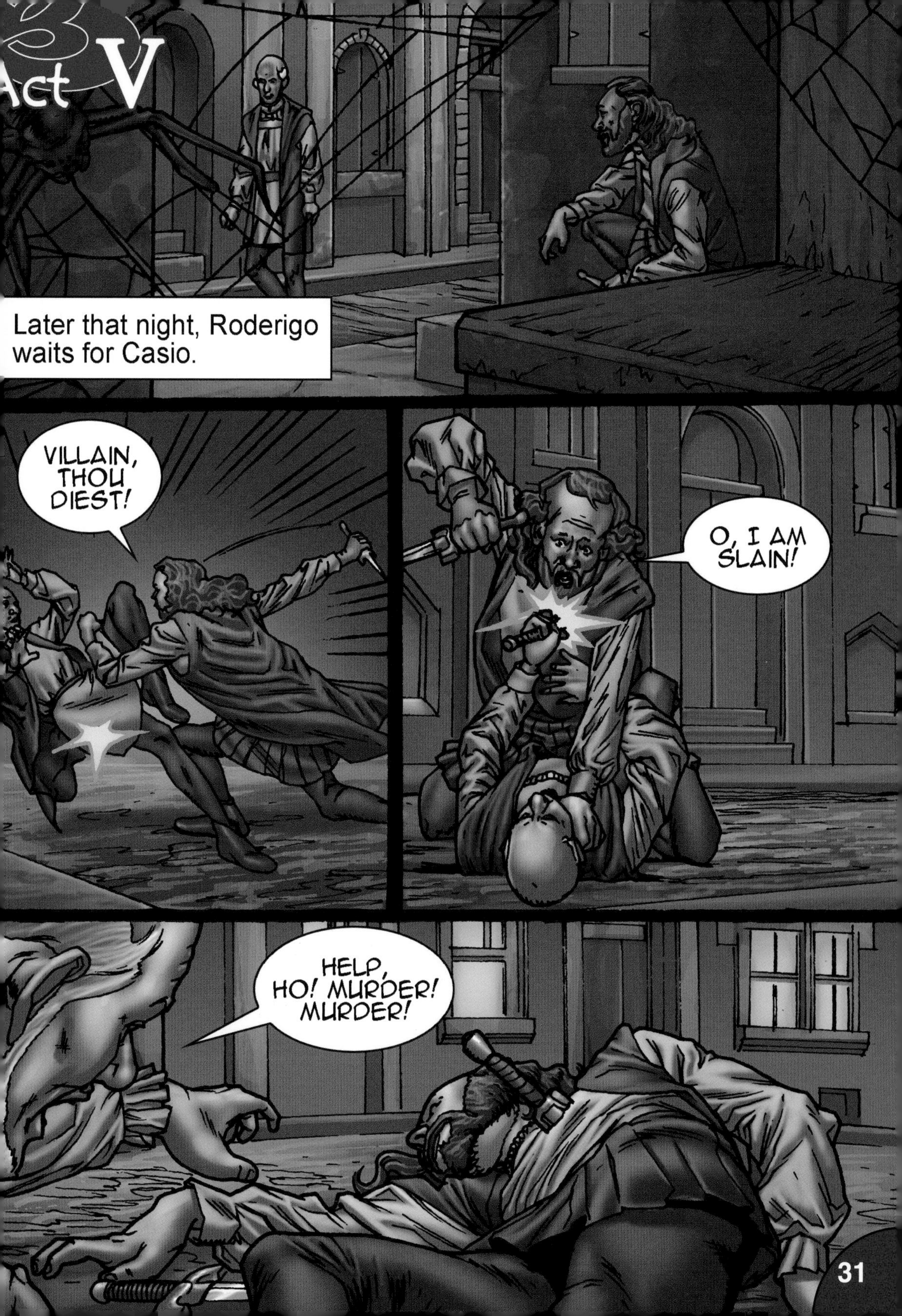
Act V
Later that night, Roderigo waits for Casio.
VILLAIN, THOU DIEST!
O, I AM SLAIN!
HELP, HO! MURDER! MURDER!

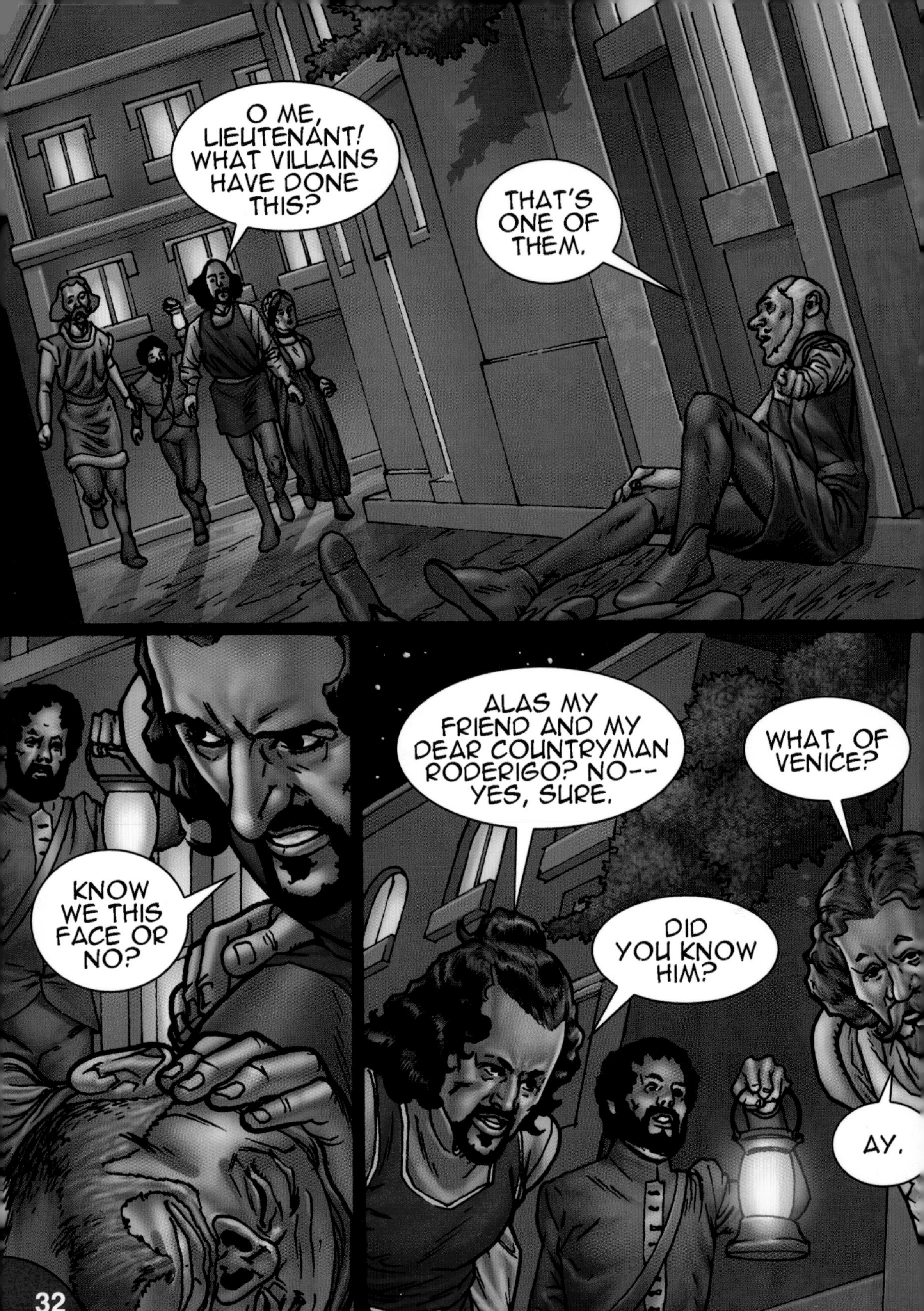
O ME, LIEUTENANT! WHAT VILLAINS HAVE DONE THIS?
THAT'S ONE OF THEM.
KNOW WE THIS FACE OR NO?
ALAS MY FRIEND AND MY DEAR COUNTRYMAN RODERIGO? NO-- YES, SURE.
WHAT, OF VENICE?
DID YOU KNOW HIM?
AY.

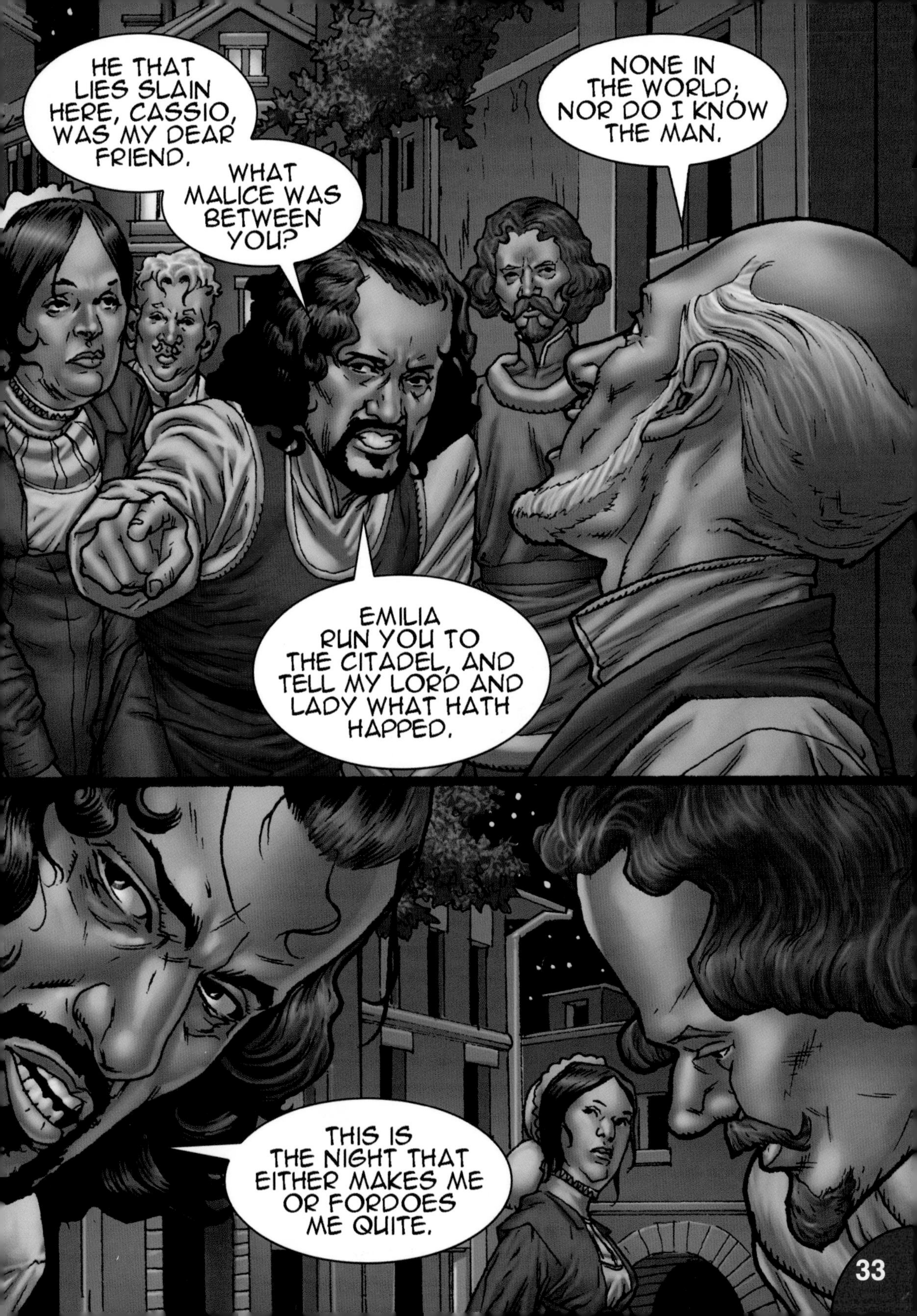
HE THAT LIES SLAIN HERE, CASSIO, WAS MY DEAR FRIEND.
WHAT MALICE WAS BETWEEN YOU?
NONE IN THE WORLD; NOR DO I KNOW THE MAN.
EMILIA RUN YOU TO THE CITADEL, AND TELL MY LORD AND LADY WHAT HATH HAPPED.
THIS IS THE NIGHT THAT EITHER MAKES ME OR FORDOES ME QUITE.

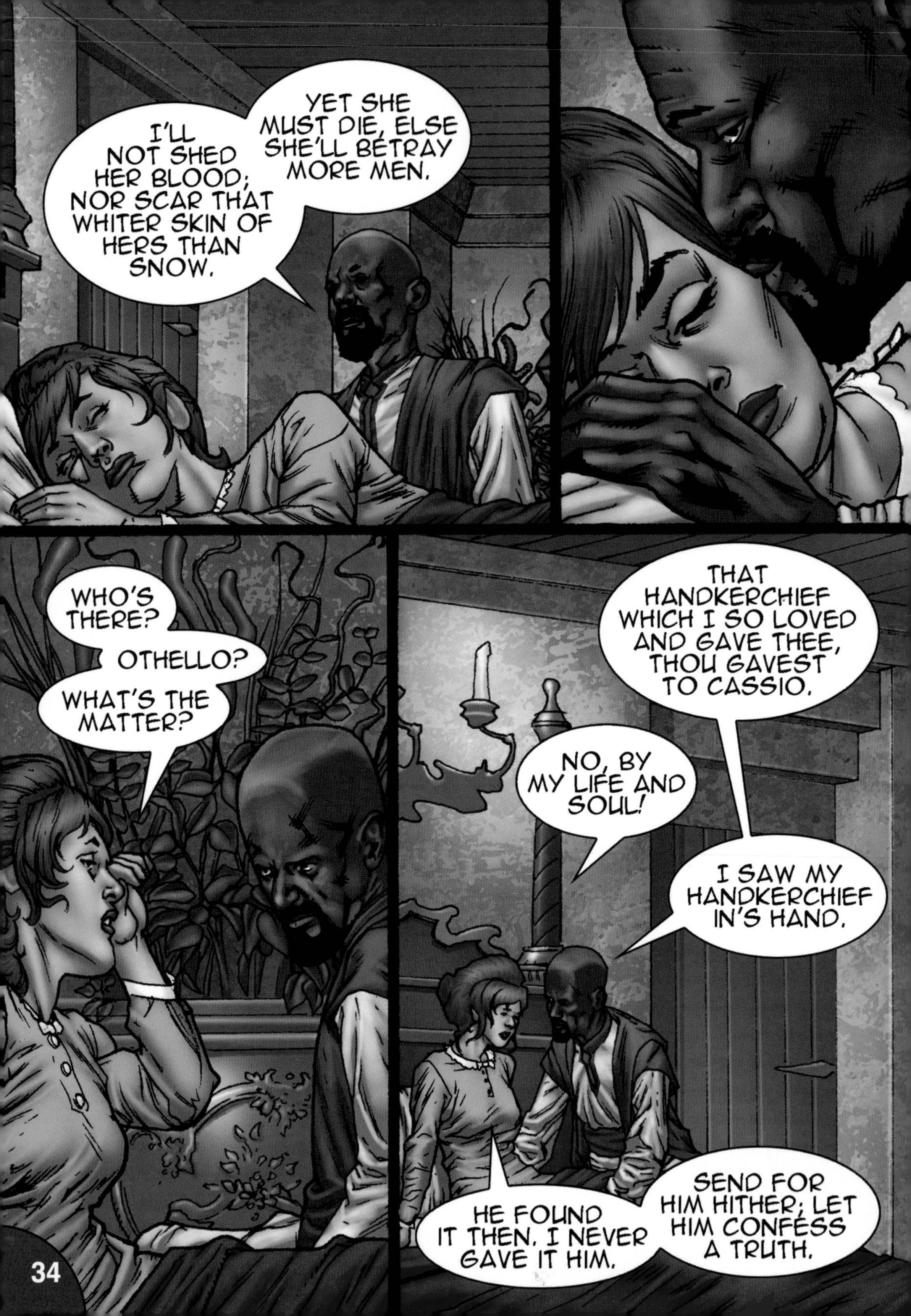

I'LL NOT SHED HER BLOOD; NOR SCAR THAT WHITER SKIN OF HERS THAN SNOW.
YET SHE MUST DIE, ELSE SHE'LL BETRAY MORE MEN.
WHO'S THERE?
OTHELLO?
WHAT'S THE MATTER?
THAT HANDKERCHIEF WHICH I SO LOVED AND GAVE THEE, THOU GAVEST TO CASSIO.
NO, BY MY LIFE AND SOUL!
I SAW MY HANDKERCHIEF IN'S HAND.
HE FOUND IT THEN. I NEVER GAVE IT HIM.
SEND FOR HIM HITHER; LET HIM CONFESS A TRUTH.

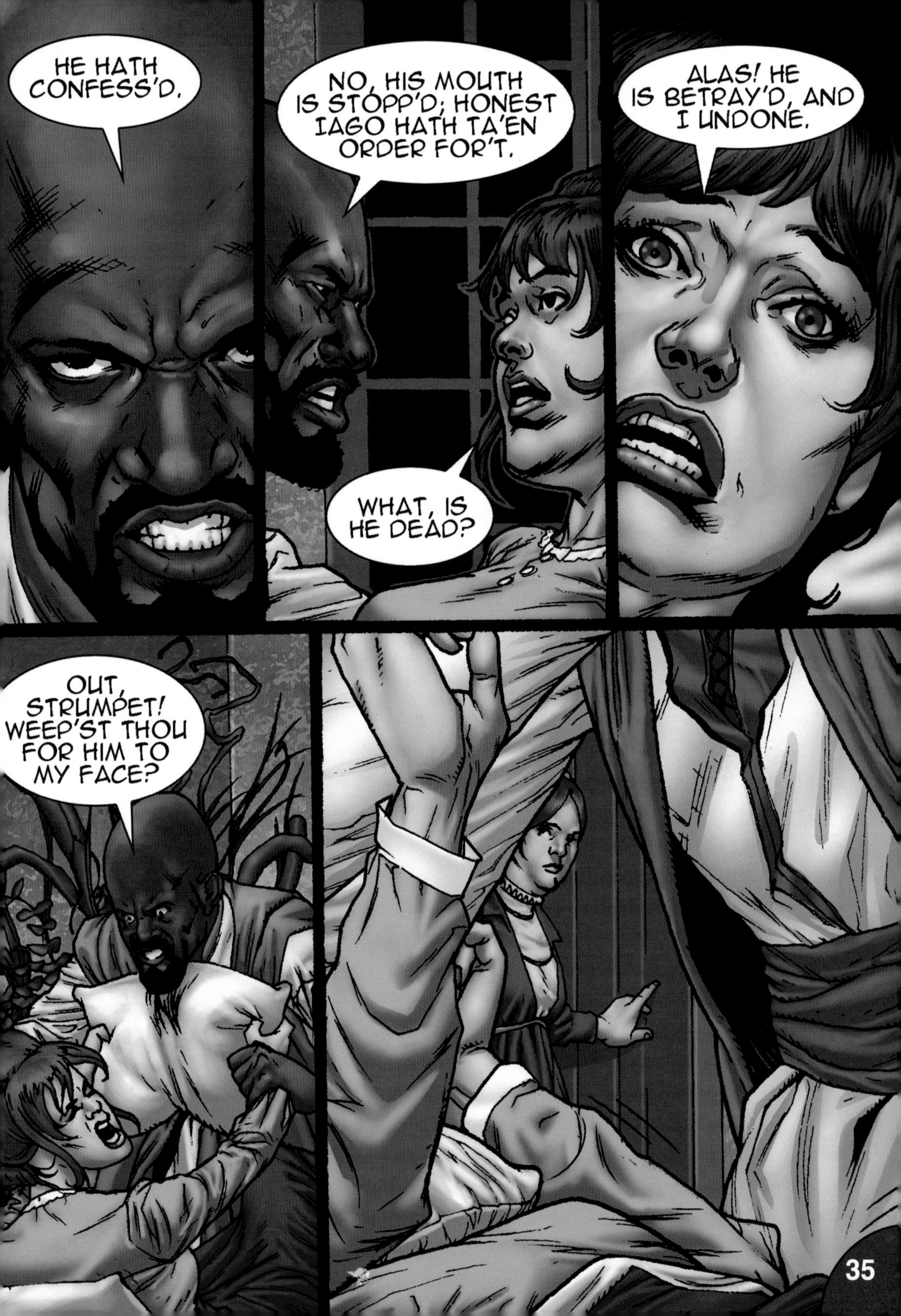
HE HATH CONFESS'D.
NO, HIS MOUTH IS STOPP'D; HONEST IAGO HATH TA'EN ORDER FOR'T.
WHAT, IS HE DEAD?
ALAS! HE IS BETRAY'D, AND I UNDONE.
OUT, STRUMPET! WEEP'ST THOU FOR HIM TO MY FACE?

37

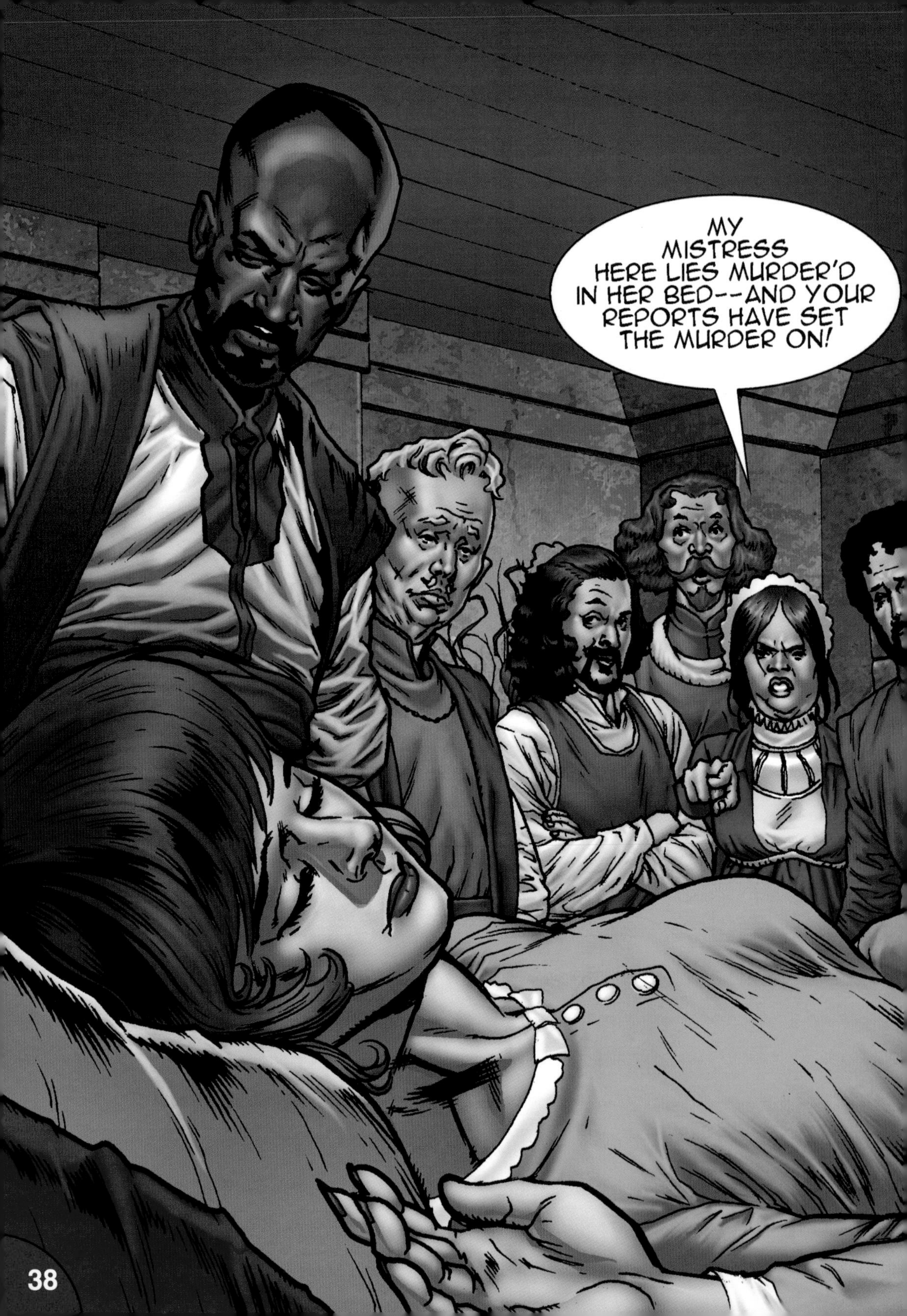
MY MISTRESS HERE LIES MURDER'D IN HER BED--AND YOUR REPORTS HAVE SET THE MURDER ON!

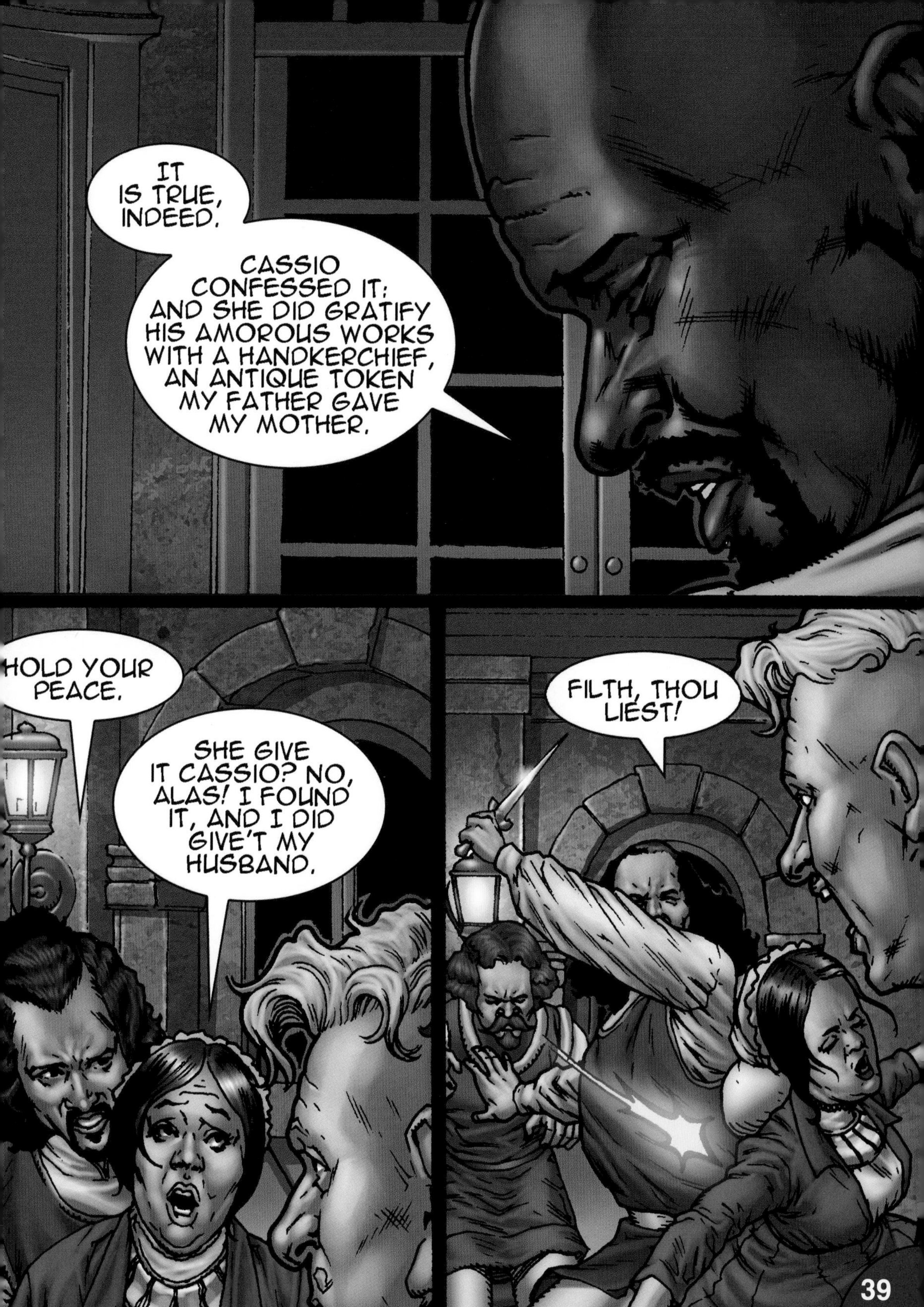
IT IS TRUE, INDEED.
CASSIO CONFESSED IT: AND SHE DID GRATIFY HIS AMOROUS WORKS WITH A HANDKERCHIEF, AN ANTIQUE TOKEN MY FATHER GAVE MY MOTHER.
HOLD YOUR PEACE.
SHE GIVE IT CASSIO? NO, ALAS! I FOUND IT, AND I DID GIVE'T MY HUSBAND.
FILTH, THOU LIEST!

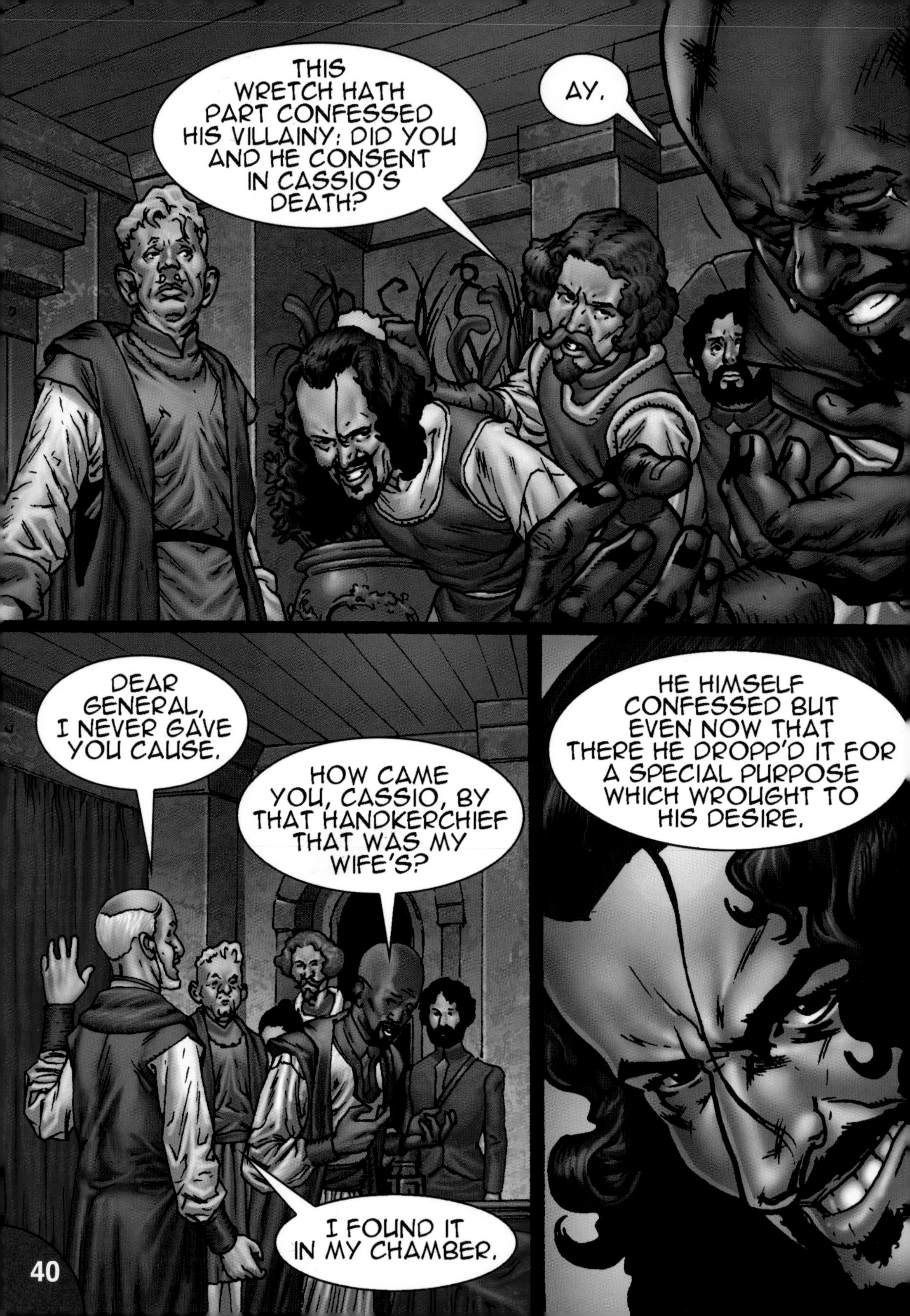
THIS WRETCH HATH PART CONFESSED HIS VILLAINY: DID YOU AND HE CONSENT IN CASSIO'S DEATH?
AY.
DEAR GENERAL, I NEVER GAVE YOU CAUSE.
HOW CAME YOU, CASSIO, BY THAT HANDKERCHIEF THAT WAS MY WIFE'S?
I FOUND IT IN MY CHAMBER.
HE HIMSELF CONFESSED BUT EVEN NOW THAT THERE HE DROPP'D IT FOR A SPECIAL PURPOSE WHICH WROUGHT TO HIS DESIRE.

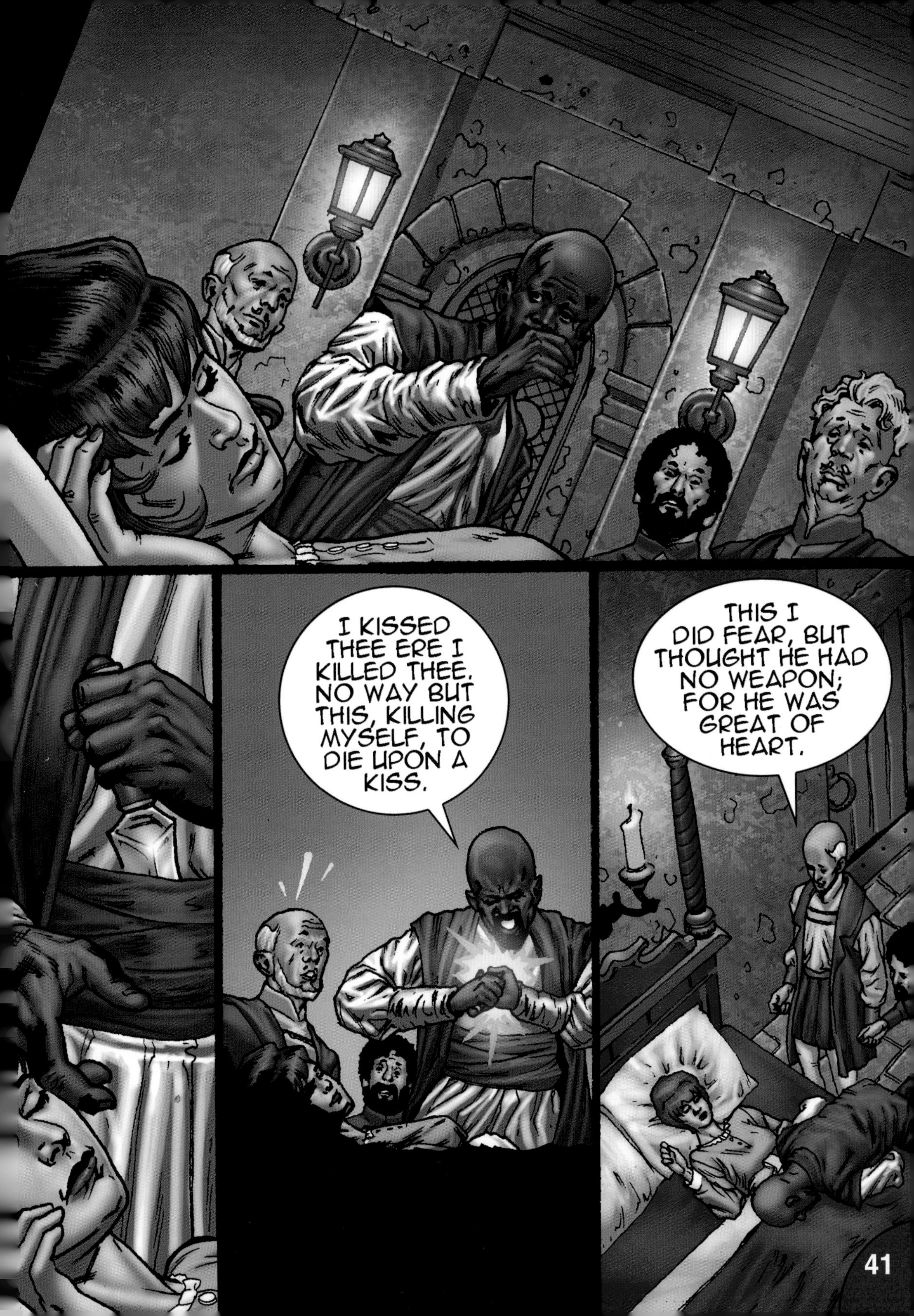
I KISSED THEE ERE I KILLED THEE. NO WAY BUT THIS, KILLING MYSELF, TO DIE UPON A KISS.
THIS I DID FEAR, BUT THOUGHT HE HAD NO WEAPON; FOR HE WAS GREAT OF HEART.

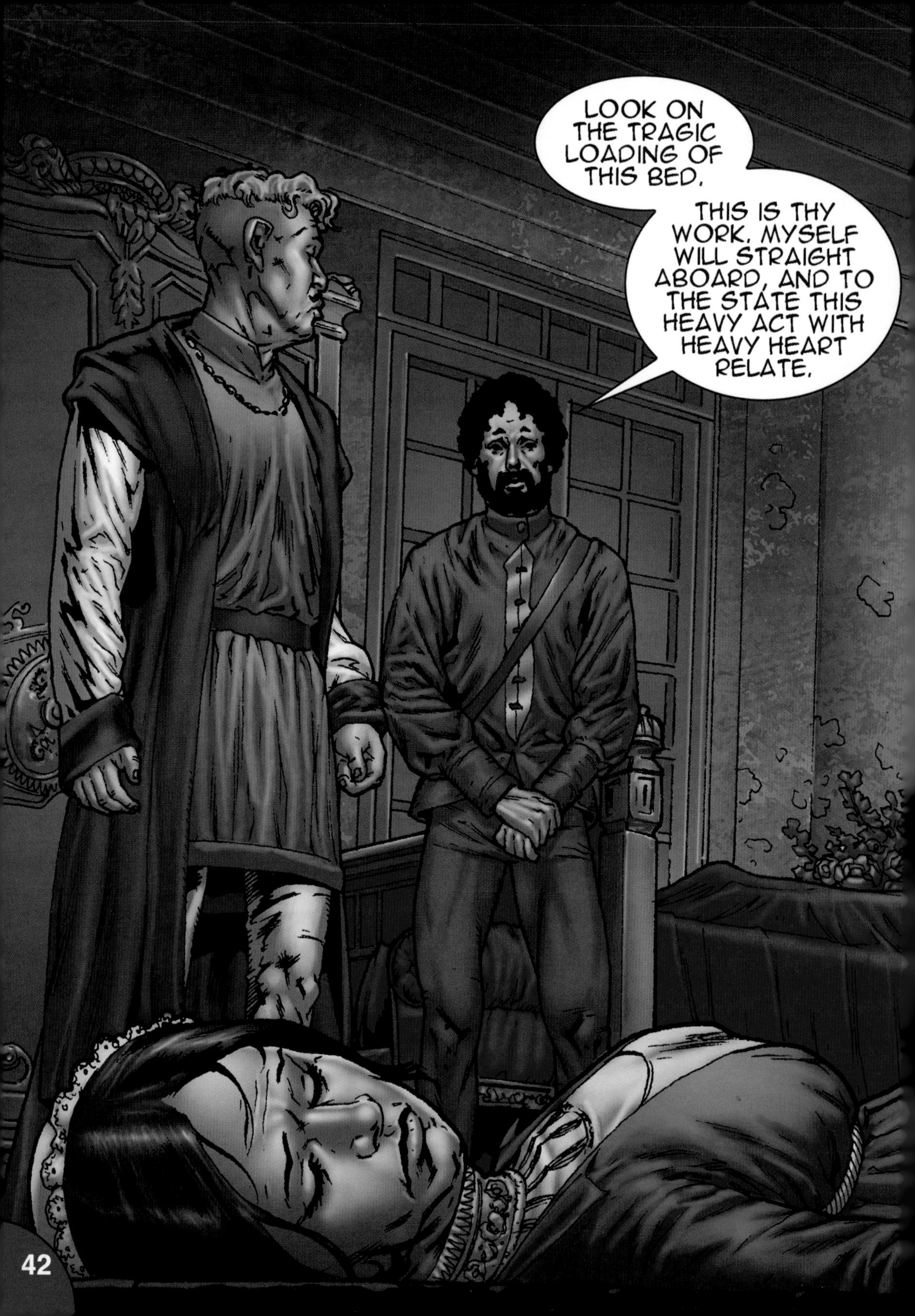
LOOK ON THE TRAGIC LOADING OF THIS BED.
THIS IS THY WORK. MYSELF WILL STRAIGHT ABOARD, AND TO THE STATE THIS HEAVY ACT WITH HEAVY HEART RELATE.

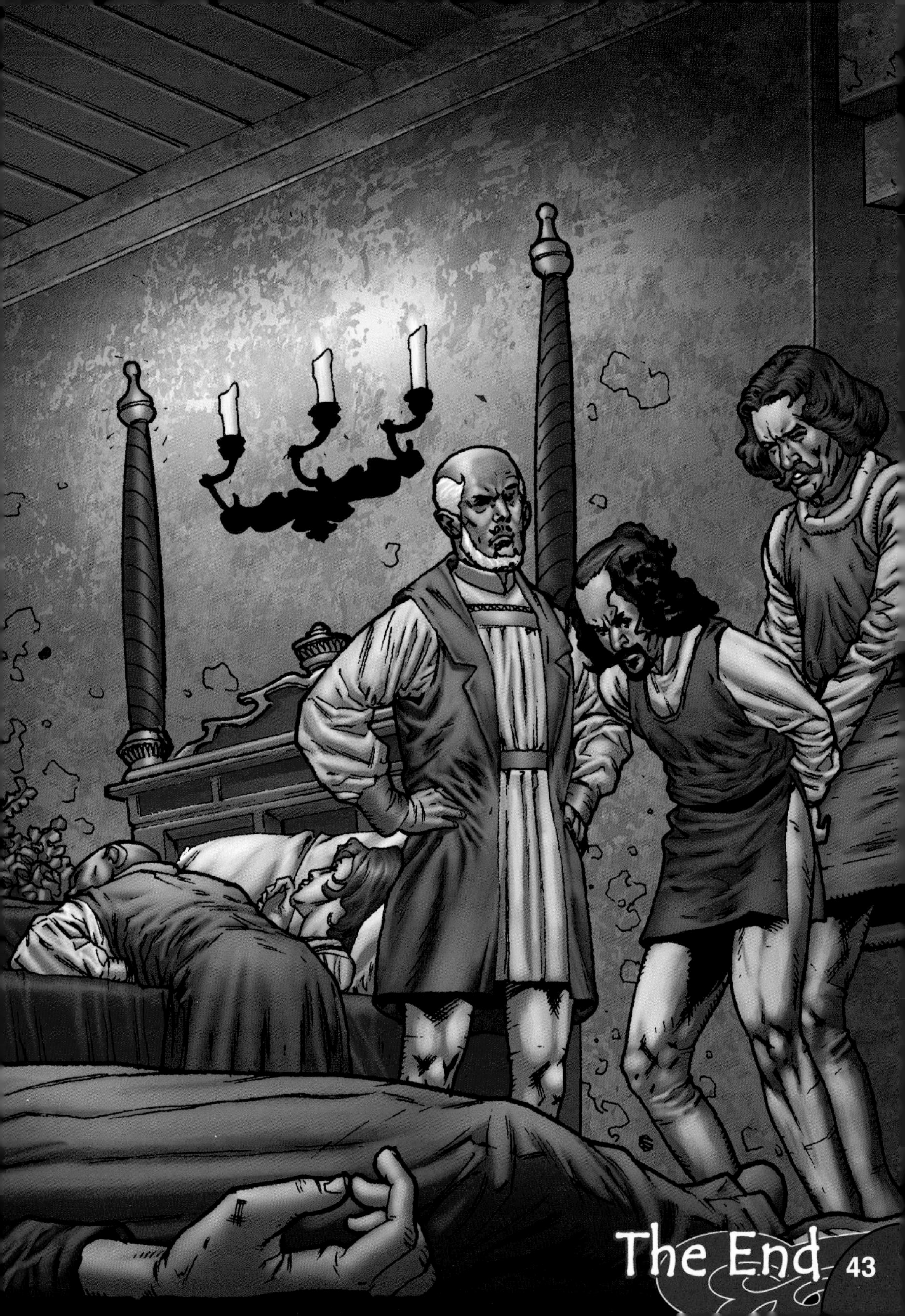
The End

Behind Othello

William Shakespeare wrote *Othello* from 1603 to 1604. The five-act tragedy was first published in 1622. It was published again in 1623 as part of Shakespeare's *First Folio*. The full title of the play is *Othello, the Moor of Venice*.

Shakespeare based Othello on an Italian tale called *De gli Hecatommithi*, written by Giambattista Giraldi. Shakespeare added supporting characters to the plot, and he set the story during a military conflict. He also made Iago the major villain.

The plot of Othello revolves around jealousy. The play opens with Othello, a general in the armies of Venice, appointing Cassio as chief lieutenant. Jealous of both Othello and Cassio, Iago plots Othello's downfall. He leads Othello to think that his wife, Desdemona, has been unfaithful to him with Cassio.

Iago uses Emilia, his wife, and Roderigo, who is in love with Desdemona, to carry out his plan. He asks Emilia to bring him Desdemona's handkerchief, which was a gift from Othello. He places the handkerchief in Cassio's room and convinces Othello that Desdemona gave it to Cassio.

Overcome with jealousy, Othello kills Desdemona. Later, Othello finds out from Emilia that Desdemona was innocent and the entire scheme was set up by Iago. Iago kills Emilia, and Othello takes his own life, ending the tragedy.

Othello was first performed in 1604 by the King's Men. The King's Men was Shakespeare's acting troupe for the court of King James I. Since then, the play has been performed throughout the world. Othello continues to be one of Shakespeare's greatest tragedies.

Famous Phrases

I am not what I am.

I will wear my heart upon my sleeve for daws to peek at.

O, beware, my lord, of jealousy; it is the green-eyed monster, which doth mock the meat that it feeds on.

Reputation, reputation, reputation! O, I have lost my reputation!

About the Author

William Shakespeare was baptized on April 26, 1564, in Stratford-upon-Avon, England. At the time, records were not kept of births, however, the churches did record baptisms, weddings, and deaths. So, we know approximately when he was born. Traditionally, his birth is celebrated on April 23.

William was the son of John Shakespeare, a tradesman, and Mary Arden. He most likely attended grammar school and learned to read, write, and speak Latin.

Shakespeare did not go on to the university. Instead, he married Anne Hathaway at age 18. They had three children, Susanna, Hamnet, and Judith. Not much is known about Shakespeare's life at this time. By 1592 he had moved to London, and his name began to appear in the literary world.

In 1594, Shakespeare became an important member of Lord Chamberlain's company of players. This group had the best actors and the best theater, the Globe. For the next 20 years, Shakespeare devoted himself to writing. He died on April 23, 1616, but his works have lived on.

Additional Works by Shakespeare

The Comedy of Errors (1589–94)
The Taming of the Shrew (1590–94)
Romeo and Juliet (1594–96)
A Midsummer Night's Dream (1595–96)
Much Ado About Nothing (1598–99)
As You Like It (1598–1600)
Hamlet (1599–1601)
Twelfth Night (1600–02)
Othello (1603–04)
King Lear (1605–06)
Macbeth (1606–07)
The Tempest (1611)

About the Adapters

Vincent Goodwin earned his B.A. in Drama and Communications om Trinity University in San Antonio. He is the writer of three ays as well as the co-writer of the comic book *Pirates vs. Ninjas* Goodwin is also an accomplished journalist, having won several wards for his work as a columnist and reporter.

Christopher Allen was born February 19, 1972 in New York City nd grew up in Winter Park, Florida. He attended Winter Park High chool, where he developed an interest in art, and in comic art in articular. His first work for ABDO was illustrating the biography of eorge Washington Carver.

Glossary

citadel - a city's fortress.

cuckold - a man whose wife is unfaithful.

durst - dare.

haste-posthaste - hurry with great speed.

hearted - deeply felt in one's heart.

mazzard - head.

minx - wanton.

mutualities - exchanges.

ocular - based on what is seen.

odd-even - midnight, the time when it is difficult to tell one day from the next.

pestilence - a dangerous disease.

prithee - a way to make a request.

rheum - watering of the eyes.

rogue - a dishonest or worthless person.

Web Sites

To learn more about William Shakespeare, visit ABDO Publishing Company on the World Wide Web at **www.abdopublishing.com**. Web sites about Shakespeare are featured on our Book Links page. These links are routinely monitored and updated to provide the most current information available.